WILD CARDS AND WITCHES

PANDORA'S PRIDE, BOOK 4

ANNABEL CHASE

RED PALM PRESS LLC

CHAPTER ONE

I STOOD outside the wooden gates for the seventh day in a row. The gate was high enough to block any view of the village on the other side. The witches in Salem didn't take kindly to strangers. History had taught them to be wary of outsiders and they'd taken that lesson to heart, erecting a physical barrier around the village as well as a magical one. I'd tested the ward on the second day of my arrival and decided it was best to wait. If I showed them I was determined, eventually they'd cave.

I hoped.

"Hungry?"

I turned to see Nathaniel behind me. The werewolf held a crisp red apple in his palm. "Lots of orchards around here. I was spoiled for choice."

"And probably stealing, too." Despite my suspicion, I accepted the apple and took a generous bite.

"Anyone leave this morning?" he asked.

"Not yet, but my money's on Amity," I said. The teenaged witch seemed to serve as the coven's errand girl.

Nathaniel gave me a pointed look. "Amity isn't going to waver."

"Oh, I know, but I figure she might trip on her way out and leave the ward vulnerable for that extra second."

He chuckled. "And what? You'll leap over her fallen body and barge your way in?"

"Something like that." I took another bite of the apple and relished the sweet, juicy taste.

Nathaniel shook his head. "Not you, Callie. I know you better than that. You'd help her up first and make sure she wasn't hurt."

He wasn't wrong. I had an innate desire to help others. I blamed my father—or the mage I thought was my father until recently. My biological parents—Greta and Quinn Wendell—died not long after I was born. I was raised by a man named Duncan Waite who'd assumed my father's identity. The revelation still burned and I shoved aside the ensuing thoughts so I could focus on the task at hand.

"You hear about breaking out of a prison, but not so much breaking in."

Nathaniel lifted his brow. "Need I remind you this is a coven village."

"Could've fooled me." I leaned against the fence and continued to chomp on the apple. The coven could try their best to keep me out, but I'd wear them down eventually. I no longer had a job or any responsibility. I had nothing but time to kill.

"Any attempts to contact you?" Nathaniel asked.

I averted my gaze. "No."

"Can't decide if you're relieved or disappointed," he said.

"Me neither." Was it possible to be both?

"I think a clean break is best, at least for now," Nathaniel said.

I agreed, although it didn't make it any easier. The

members of Pandora's Pride had become like family to me, maybe because they were—sort of. Once I made the discovery that I'd been magically imbued with the traits of all five species of the Pride's inner circle, it was difficult to know how to categorize them. They'd employed me. Befriended me.

Betrayed me.

I melted against the fence, thinking of Saxon. He didn't know the truth. He had to be confused and upset by my disappearance. Tate and Liam, too. Even Evadne. They had no clue as to my real identity. I wondered whether they suspected anything about themselves. Not Tate, of course. She was Abra's granddaughter and, therefore, too precious to experiment on. Not me. I was expendable—until I became their only true success story. Now I was coveted, but only as a dangerous weapon to wield in the war against Plague demons.

The gate creaked and I shifted to an alert position, chucking the apple over my shoulder. Amity slipped between the gap in the gate, toting a wicker basket. The coven had clearly decided we weren't a threat because they continued to send Amity out each morning regardless of our presence. Today she wore her blond hair in two braids, each one laced with a white ribbon.

"Good morning, Calandra. Nathaniel." Amity offered a hesitant smile.

"Morning, Amity," Nathaniel said.

"Let me guess," I said. "You've come to tell us that your fearless leader has decided to welcome us with open arms."

Amity looked down at the ground. "You know we don't welcome outsiders."

"I already told you—I'm not an outsider. I'm one of you."

Amity chewed her lip. "Marie says that's not possible."

3

"I'm sure she does. Tell her I would've agreed with her a couple months ago, but I've learned a few things since then."

Nathaniel snorted. "Leave the girl be, Callie. She has chores to do."

"I'm not harassing her." I turned to look at the witch. "Am I harassing you?"

She lowered her head. "No, miss."

"You're getting old," Nathaniel said. "She called you 'miss.'"

I shrugged. "Hey, at least it wasn't ma'am."

"Would you like an apple, Amity?" Nathaniel asked.

I frowned. "I think the witch is supposed to offer the apple to the innocent party, not the other way around."

"No thank you," Amity said. "I've already eaten."

The witch continued walking but I glimpsed the hint of a smile as she turned away.

"Maybe they're testing us," I said, once Amity was out of earshot.

"Oh, I definitely think they're testing us."

I smiled. "Not like that. I mean, they won't let us in and we keep hanging out here anyway. What's to stop us from grabbing Amity and using her as leverage to enter?"

"Amity's young and being tasked with errands. Maybe they view her as disposable."

I winced. Another young woman who seemingly didn't matter. I would expect better from a coven.

"You might want to consider a different tack," Nathaniel said. "You can't stand out here forever."

I circled my shoulders to loosen the muscles. We'd been sleeping rough all week and the absence of a warm bed was taking a toll, at least on me. I'd spent most of my life sleeping outdoors in the Rocky Mountains. You'd think I could handle a week in Massachusetts, especially when it wasn't even winter yet. Nathaniel had accused me of getting soft during my time in Atlantica City. If it weren't for all the training and fighting I did while I was there, I might've been inclined to agree with him.

I leaned my forehead against the fence and listened for movement on the other side. A few of the younger witches sometimes came to whisper and giggle. They weren't skilled enough to break through the ward, but I had a feeling if they were, they would've sent over a couple of toads just to mess with us. Ah, kids. They were the same in any species.

A gust of wind blew past us, scattering golden leaves in the air. It was a beautiful image, like watching a sunburst.

"Good thing her dress goes all the way to her ankles or Amity might be showing the town her underpants," I said, although right now her exposure would be limited to the trees and a host of woodland creatures.

Another rush of wind kicked up dirt as well as leaves. I glanced at the sky, which was a solid sheet of blue. Not a cloud in sight.

"It almost feels like a storm is brewing," I said.

Nathaniel sniffed the air. "I don't smell rain."

The back of my neck pricked. "Something's wrong."

He shot me a quizzical look. "Vamp?"

I shook my head. "No." I glanced at the path Amity had taken through the forest. "I think we should follow her."

Nathaniel nodded mutely and we abandoned our posts. The forest was strangely silent as we stepped onto the path. No birdsong. No chittering. It seemed like the calm before the storm.

A blast of air streaked through the trees and sent twigs and leaves flying in all directions. Nathaniel ducked to avoid getting knocked in the head by a particularly thick branch. He and I exchanged looks of alarm. This wasn't Mother Nature's work.

A scream pierced the air and I rushed forward. The wind

grew stronger the deeper into the woods I went and I squinted to keep the debris out of my eyes. Ahead of me mighty oak trees bent and twisted.

"Amity," I yelled.

Another scream answered me.

I leaped over a fallen tree and into a clearing where a cyclone had formed. It was about twenty feet tall and eight feet in circumference. The handle of Amity's basket was stuck to a nearby bush. I gasped in horror when I realized that Amity was trapped inside the maelstrom.

Nathaniel joined me at the clearing. "A matangi demon?"

I nodded. I hadn't seen one of these in a long time. The 'whirlwind' demons had more of a presence in the woods of the Pacific Northwest, but a couple had made their way to the forests of the Rocky Mountains over the years. Apparently, some had made their way all the way to the East Coast.

"I'll leave this one to you," he said.

"That would be wise." A werewolf was no good in a fight with a matangi demon, not when magic was required. Although Amity was a witch, she was young and the coven likely had no experience with this type of demon.

Whatever I did, I had to be careful not to injure Amity in the process. That meant no fire magic, not that I would use that in a forest anyway. I decided to play it safe. I pulled an enchanted Wild Card from my pocket and focused on the demon.

"Inertia," I said.

Nothing happened. Okay, this demon required more than a basic enchantment. I tapped into my elemental magic. The matangi demon was essentially made of wind, and if I could manipulate air…

I concentrated on the demon and tugged. Hard.

I didn't want to pull the entire cyclone toward me. Instead, I wanted to unravel it like a spool of yarn.

This time I yanked from the opposite direction that the cyclone was spinning. The whirlwind collapsed in on itself like a dying star and a wall of wind blasted away from it in a circle. The force knocked me off my feet but I quickly recovered. I spotted Amity in a heap in the center of the clearing and raced to crouch by her side.

"Amity." I touched her shoulder, afraid to move her in any way. I didn't want to exacerbate any injuries.

The young witch blinked. "Am I dead?"

I laughed. "Nobody would dare put me in charge of greeting shades in the afterlife. Are you hurt?"

Slowly, she pulled herself into a seated position. "Sore."

"That's understandable. You got sucked into a whirlwind demon."

She looked at me and frowned. "That was a demon?"

I nodded. "I take it you've never encountered one of those before."

"No." She hesitated. "I've never encountered any demons before."

I balked. "Never? Not even a feral vampire?"

"Only the occasional wolf," Amity said, "but I know a spell to keep them at bay." She gave Nathaniel a guilty look. "No offense, sir."

I helped Amity to her feet. "Maybe you should skip errands today. I'm sure Marie will understand."

"You are correct," a voice interjected. "Marie understands."

I twisted to see Marie with five other witches fanned out behind her. Her sun-kissed skin rippled with signs of age and her white hair was pulled into a thick braid. She wore a plain grey dress that brushed the forest floor. The only sign of her authority was the jewelry around her neck—a hazelnut, which signified her divine insight and magical knowledge.

"It's not what it looks like," I said quickly. If the coven

7

thought for one second that I'd hurt Amity, my chance to talk to them would vanish in the air like the whirlwind.

"We know," Marie said. "We were alerted to the presence of the demon, but a little too late, it seems." The witch shifted her attention to Amity. "You may continue your duties. There was only one demon detected and it's clearly no longer an issue."

Amity tugged her basket free of the bushes and bowed respectfully before hurrying away.

"You're welcome," I called after her.

Marie clasped her hands in front of her. "Come with me, Calandra Wendell."

My brow lifted. "Don't worry. I'm not going to follow her. If you say there's only one demon, then I believe you."

"And if you say you are one of us, *I* believe *you*." She turned and left the clearing with her entourage directly behind her.

I cut a quick glance at Nathaniel. "What just happened?"

"Congratulations. I think you've earned her trust."

I scurried after the witches, my heart pounding in my chest. Hallelujah! All my stubborn stalking was about to pay off.

When we reached the gate, the witches let me pass but blocked Nathaniel's path.

Marie turned to address him. "Not you, I'm afraid."

Nathaniel bowed his head. "Understood."

I gave the werewolf a cheerful thumbs up before trailing after Marie.

The village was more primitive than I expected, a far cry from the decadence of the hotels and casinos in Atlantica City. The land was dotted with thatched-roof cottages, extensive herb gardens, and even a blacksmith shop.

"I feel like I'm stepping back in time," I said.

Marie stopped walking and waited for me to catch up.

"This place was intended as an interpretation of early life in Salem. A living museum created by humans. Ironic that it now serves as our true home."

"What happened to the humans?"

"They abandoned Salem and most of Boston after the Plague and we reclaimed this entire area all the way to the Berkshires, one of the few bright spots of that unfortunate event."

"Why not stay in Boston?" I asked. Although it wouldn't have the same level of sophistication as a pre-Plague city, Boston would still have a slew of advantages over a rudimentary village.

Marie surveyed the village with a satisfied smile. "The forest. The ocean. So much magical energy surrounds us here. No, this is home."

Looking around at the well-kept cottages and the little girls running amok in their dresses, I felt a sense of peace wash over me.

A witch rounded the corner of one of the cottages and bowed her head.

"The Stone House is ready, Marie," she said.

"Excellent, Ophelia. Thank you." She turned to me. "I thought it best to talk there. It's the better option in the village for private conversations."

"Because it's made of stone?"

She wore a vague smile. "Because it's under a spell that prevents eavesdropping."

Everyone had secrets they wanted to keep, it seemed. Abra had come by her methods honestly.

The Stone House was exactly as described. The building was smaller than the cottages and the interior contained fewer amenities than my hotel room at Salt.

"This building was designed for meetings only," Marie said, seeming to notice my reaction. "No one ever lived here."

She gestured to a brown leather chair opposite a coffee table. "Please, sit."

Marie sat opposite me and a knock on the door interrupted us. A witch nudged open the door with a teapot and two cups on a tray.

"Shall I leave it by the door?" the witch asked.

She looked slightly younger than Amity, with a single red braid hanging down her back and a smattering of freckles across the bridge of her nose. Seeing all these basic witches made me wonder when and how Abra had adopted her elegant fashion sense. Nobody in this village would be caught wearing pearls.

"The table, please, Helena," Marie said.

Helena took her time crossing the room with the tray and I got the sense that she'd suffered a delivery mishap in the recent past.

"Is it true you're a long-lost member of our coven?" Helena asked, eyeing me with childlike curiosity.

"Her status is yet to be determined," Marie said. "I'll pour the tea. Be on your way now."

Helena hurried from the room with a final backward glance.

"She's Amity's sister," I said. Although their coloring differed, they shared the same slightly upturned nose.

"Half-sister," Marie said. "Same mother. Different fathers."

"I was wondering how you managed to add to your stable of witches. Do you invite the men inside the village once a year for a special gathering?" I used air quotes for 'special.'

Marie offered an inelegant snort. "We do nothing of the kind, although it would make for an interesting evening."

"How do you keep your numbers up?"

Marie filled each cup with tea. "You're as observant as you are powerful. You've been taught well."

"I've had a lot of teachers." More than most, in fact. "I notice you didn't answer the question."

"There's nothing exciting about the answer. The adult witches are free to go in and out of the village. Most of the time they choose to stay, but occasionally they'll get the itch to seek company."

"And the men aren't looking for a nuclear family?" I'd heard my father use that term many times during my childhood. He'd bemoan the fact that he couldn't offer me a 'nuclear family,' as though the phrase had some profound meaning and its mere existence would automatically make me a better person.

"What is it that brings you to us?" Marie asked, ignoring my question. Small talk was over, apparently.

"I want to ask you about a witch from your coven called Abra."

Marie's eyes flashed with disdain. "Abra? You should have told me that from the first day."

"Because you would've let me in sooner?"

Her expression hardened. "Because I would have sent you away sooner."

"That popular, huh?"

Marie raised a cup to her lips and sipped. "I try not to think of her."

I scrutinized Marie's face—the thinness of her pale pink lips and the shape of her eyes. "Abra is *your* sister."

Marie smiled and set down her cup. "Half-sister."

Mind. Blown.

"Tate has the same eye shape, too," I said. I took a grateful sip of tea. I'd been forced to break my coffee habit when I left Atlantica City and hot drinks had been few and far between on the road.

The wrinkles in Marie's brow deepened. "Who is Tate?"

"Her granddaughter."

Marie looked toward the door, smiling sadly. "Abra and I haven't spoken in many years. I know nothing of her grandchildren."

"What caused the rift?" I asked.

"A combination of factors," Marie said vaguely. "Abra and I didn't always see eye-to-eye on how to handle coven business."

"And you were both in charge? Like joint bosses?"

She chuckled. "Only after our mother passed. If you want to see true strength, I'll show you an old photograph."

"I guess that's a trait you admire. Is that why you decided to let me in—because I was strong enough to save Amity?" I took another drink and relished the warmth of the liquid as it coated my mouth and throat. I'd never take coffee or tea for granted again.

Marie angled her head. "Is that what you think?"

Confusion muddied my thoughts. "You don't think I saved her?"

"Oh, I know you saved her. I saw it happen with my own two eyes, but that alone would not have been enough."

I peered at her over the top of my cup. "Then what?"

"I saw the spell you conjured to defeat the demon," Marie said. "Only a witch of our provenance could have summoned forth that kind of magic."

"It was a simple spell," I argued.

She laughed. "Who told you that? I have witches born and raised in this village that haven't mastered it."

"Are you saying you believe me?" I set down my cup in disbelief. I thought it would be a harder sell.

Marie examined me closely. "I believe that you have somehow learned to access our power."

"Not just yours. Everybody's." I opened my arms wide. "I'm the whole enchilada."

"What does that mean?"

"It means I'm a supernatural sundae. I'm a little bit of you, with a dab of angel, a scoop of vampire, a dollop of fae, and topped with werewolf sprinkles."

I realized that telling her wouldn't be enough. I was going to have to flaunt the goods. I rose to my feet and willed my wings to appear.

Marie jumped at the sight of them. "I don't understand."

I adopted my best game show host voice. "But wait. There's more." I focused on my mouth and felt the fangs slide into position. I'd spent the past couple weeks with Nathaniel honing my skills. Now that I knew who I was—and what I was—I was better able to grasp my potential.

"Fangs," she whispered, mildly horrified. "Like a vampire."

I plucked one of the fangs with my fingers. "Not just for show either. These babies have been tested."

Marie tilted her head in amazement. "How can one possibly be all of these things?"

"You'll have to ask your sister about that."

The witch gaped at me. "Abra is…responsible?"

"You sound surprised. I thought maybe that's the reason you parted ways. She wanted to use Franken-magic and you had scruples."

Marie lifted her cup back to her mouth and I noticed a slight tremble in her hands. "That was not one of our differences, although it certainly would have been had the suggestion ever been made."

"She ran magical experiments on children," I said. "Some orphans. Some abandoned."

Marie downed the rest of her tea as though her cup was filled with tequila. "Children," she whispered.

"She didn't do it alone. She had the help of other species down at the farm and I'm their prize pig."

Marie shook her head, trying to process the information. "And how did they create this powerful combined magic?"

"I don't know the spells they used," I said truthfully. "There was a lot of trial and error." I didn't mention their use of the Sunstone. The powerful gemstone was now back in the Pride's possession and I thought it best to keep its existence to myself.

"I knew she wanted to take a radical approach to battling Plague demons," Marie said, trailing off.

"And you disagreed with her approach?"

"My sister wanted to join forces with other species. Our coven had always been insular and I believed we had a better chance of survival if we remained so. Abra was insistent that the way forward was an alliance with the other main species to fight together against the demons."

"Did she have a species in mind at the time or was she speaking hypothetically?"

"She was friends with an angel she'd met at a leadership conference before the Plague. I believe they developed the idea together."

"Doran," I said.

Marie snapped to attention. "Yes. He's involved in this?"

"He's the reason I can dream walk and do all sorts of other fun activities."

Marie returned her cup to the table and leaned against her chair, appearing shell-shocked by the news. "It seems my sister went far beyond what she'd first envisioned as her plan to defeat the demons."

"Were you not concerned?" I asked.

"Of course I was," she said indignantly. "The witches suffered greatly during the Plague. It was a horrific time for the coven."

"People still suffer," I said. "The whole world still suffers."

"Yes, but it's an occasional flareup rather than constant terror."

I polished off the rest of my tea and set the cup on the

tray. "I think that depends on your location. I've seen quite a lot of destruction and devastation."

"You've been fighting them then? Acting as Abra's magical foot soldier?"

"Something like that," I said. I didn't want to get into the details of my past. They weren't necessary to this conversation.

"And you work in conjunction with other species?"

"Yes. Two hybrids and a tri-brid, as well as Tate."

Marie recoiled. "Abra sends her own granddaughter into battle?"

"Tate is very capable, even without the traits of other supernaturals," I said.

"And it works...well?"

"Honestly, the main thing we have going for us is that Plague demons will never work together." They weren't cooperative or collaborative in their approach to anything ever. If they were, the world would be in even deeper trouble than it already was.

Marie met my gaze. "You're comparing this coven with Plague demons?"

That wasn't my intention, but now that she mentioned it...

"We're stronger together," I said. "I might not agree with Abra's solution to the problem, but I agree with that part."

She gave me an appraising look. "You remind me of her. Strange to say, I realize."

"Not that strange all things considered," I admitted.

Her gaze became so intense that I momentarily lost the power of speech.

"You're angry with my sister," she finally said.

"Yes. She had no right to use us. We had no voice. No choice."

"How old were you when this was done to you?" Marie asked.

"An infant," I said.

Marie blew out a soft breath. "A babe. And what is it that you seek from us now?"

"Information. Abra is going to come for me sooner or later. She let me get away once and I know she won't let it happen again. The Pride needs me."

"But it sounds as though you want to fight the Plague demons?"

"I do, but I don't agree with her methods. I want to find another way." A way that didn't involve stripping innocent children of their rights.

Marie nodded. "On that we're in complete agreement."

"Would you mind keeping our conversation between us?" I asked. "There are certain factions of supernaturals who also don't agree with her methods, but they would rather kill me than sympathize."

The witch's features were etched with concern. "Insult to injury."

"That's the way I see it."

"You're welcome to stay in the village with us as long as you like. I won't breathe a word."

"Thank you, but I can't leave Nathaniel alone. He's an older werewolf and he'll get himself in trouble without supervision."

She laughed. "Then the coven will be sure to bring you provisions. You're welcome to set up camp outside the gates." She paused, a twinkle in her eye. "Although it's fair to say you already have."

"True. I've been there all week."

Marie lifted my cup from the table.

"That's my cup," I said.

"Oh, I know." She proceeded to examine the remaining

contents.

"Really?" I hadn't pegged her as a witch who read tea leaves. I expected something grander.

"I know it might seem beneath my station," Marie said. "Abra certainly felt that way. She was more interested in raw power. My grandmother was a skilled diviner, though, and I learned from her. It was one of my favorite pastimes when I was younger."

Simpler times. Everything about this coven suggested they preferred that world to the present one. But just because they desired it didn't make it so. There was a whole world spinning in chaos, no matter how many homespun dresses they produced. They couldn't hide from the aftermath of the Plague forever, although admittedly they'd done a pretty commendable job so far.

Marie sifted the leaves from side to side, peering intently at the bottom of the cup. "Hmm."

"Is that your official statement on my future? Because it seems appropriate."

She broke into a genuine smile that quickly faded as she stared at the leaves. "Your future is uncertain."

"Hedging your bets?"

Marie shook her head. "I see three paths."

"Only three? I'm young. I feel like there should be more options."

She showed me the bottom of the cup. "Do you see this tree with three branches?"

I squinted at the specks of black. "I'll take your word for it."

"You will be confronted with choices, Calandra, and the future depends on you making the right ones."

"*My* future, you mean?"

"No, Calandra." Her expression darkened as she brought the cup to rest in her lap. "The future of us all."

CHAPTER TWO

As TEMPTED as I was by four walls and a bed, I felt too guilty to leave Nathaniel outside the village on his own. We set up camp in the woods, still within sight of the gate. I did, however, take advantage of the sink and toilet offered to me before returning to the werewolf.

I sat cross-legged on the bedroll and rubbed my hands together, prompting a groan from Nathaniel.

"Not more portal practice," he said.

I cast him a sidelong glance. "Practice makes perfect. You know that."

"But you've already gotten so good at it. Why don't you give it a rest tonight?"

I unfolded my legs. "Fine, but only because you asked nicely. I'd love to practice spells with the coven while I'm here. Maybe learn some new ones."

"You've really taken to your newfound abilities."

"I wouldn't go that far."

"Callie, you seem to focus on a trait every free minute you have."

I looked at him. "This is Abra's original coven. Marie has

accepted me. I'd be a fool not to take advantage of this opportunity."

"I'm glad you two got along, not that I'm surprised. You could charm the rattle off a snake." Nathaniel unrolled the more comfortable bedding the coven had generously provided.

"You should've seen the horror in her eyes," I said. "I can understand why Abra left. Her ideas wouldn't have been tolerated. These witches are powerful, but they don't want to use magic to fight. They prefer a simple life."

Part of me thought they were privileged to have a choice. Then again, we'd all exercised choices. Abra had made a choice, too, although hers seemed more like a necessity. She'd opted to serve a higher purpose. If the five members of the Pride hadn't banded together to prevent Plague demons from taking over the world, what would the state of affairs be now? There was no way to know for sure, but I had to imagine it would be much, much worse. I, of course, made the decision to leave Pandora's Pride and stop fighting. To not use the 'gifts' they'd granted me for the greater good. Part of me regretted it. Plague demons were out there right now, killing innocents and instead of using my abilities to stop them, I was gathering information about my former bosses. About myself.

"The line between a simple life and survival can sometimes be a thin one," Nathaniel said.

My mind was still stuck on choices and the ones I'd apparently soon be facing. "According to Marie, I'll be confronted with a choice between three paths and my decision will determine the fate of the world."

Nathaniel grunted. "No pressure then."

"I think she might be overstating it. How can one individual be that important?"

Even as the words left my mouth, I recognized my

mistake. Of course one individual could be important. Look at me. I was the lone success story and the crown jewel of Pandora's Pride. I could help them defeat every Plague demon on earth. Even more, I could help them create an entire army of super soldiers designed for the sole purpose of fighting and, quite possibly, dying. The inner circle didn't care about Callie Wendell. They cared about their invest-ment. They cared about using me to protect everyone else.

"We don't make choices in isolation," Nathaniel said. "Abra's decision to pursue a coalition with other species in spite of the coven's objections had far-reaching conse-quences, wouldn't you agree?"

Fate of the world level consequences, in fact.

Nathaniel handed me a pillow. "I bet you sleep better tonight, now that you've been inside the village."

"What makes you think I haven't been?" I fluffed the pillow.

"Oh, I don't know. The tossing. The turning. The moans of discomfort. It's like sleeping beside a geriatric princess."

I picked up the pillow and swatted at him. "You'd better watch your tongue, Nathaniel. I have dream walking abilities that could easily result in a series of nightmares for you."

"Idle threats don't scare me." He extinguished the lantern. "How long do you plan to stay here?"

"I want more information. I only scratched the surface today with Marie."

"Well, I'm glad you finally got results. I haven't seen you this upbeat since before…since we were back in the mountains."

I tucked my knees to my chest. "I haven't forgotten that he's dead, you know. You don't have to avoid saying it."

Nathaniel blew out a breath. "I didn't avoid it for you. I avoided it for me. I don't much like talking about it either."

My father had managed to make me feel safe and secure

in a world that was anything but. I had been his entire focus, I realized that now.

"He sacrificed everything for me," I said. "His career. His life."

"And he had no regrets," Nathaniel said firmly.

I straightened the sides of my bedroll. "He told me a story every single night until I was old enough to ask him to stop." I smiled at the memory of an exasperated thirteen-year-old me begging him to stop, that I was too old. What I wouldn't give to hear him tell me a story one last time.

Nathaniel stretched his long legs. "Do you have a favorite?"

"Anything with a tree." My father must've told fifty stories that involved mighty trees and I'd probably heard them at least a dozen times throughout my childhood. I suspect it was because I felt so close to nature, given the way I was raised.

"Ah, yes. I seem to recall Yggdrasil was top of your list."

"Yggdrasil," I said, smiling. "I did have a fondness for Norse stories in general."

"I believe it was Odin who captivated your interest."

I nodded. "He wasn't too masculine to practice magic. Very cool."

Odin was the leader of the Norse gods and a powerful warrior but also the master of magic, which had traditionally been associated with women. Odin didn't view magic as beneath him, however, and openly engaged in the practice of spells.

"He was also a seeker of knowledge," Nathaniel reminded me. "Sounds like someone else I know."

According to legend, Odin found enlightenment at Yggdrasil but it had required a sacrifice. His eye. Stubborn and determined, Odin was willing to do whatever it took to acquire the knowledge of the runes because he understood their value.

Another memory flashed in my mind. Nathaniel and my father seated around a campfire, laughing. I'd returned from patrol and ended up bringing back a rabbit in the process. An unexpected boon. Simple pleasures, similar to what the witches enjoyed.

"I miss our life," I said.

He took a swig from his water pouch. "Your days as a mountain guide are over, I'm afraid. You're destined for greater things whether you like it or not."

"My father wanted to protect me from greater things. He wanted me to have a normal life."

Nathaniel chuckled. "Look around. Nobody's had a normal life since the Plague, or the benchmark for normal has changed so drastically that no one recognizes it anymore."

"I thought you'd understand how I feel."

"Oh, I do." He offered me his pouch and I waved it away. "I also understand that you are one of a kind."

"We're all one of a kind."

He gave me a pointed look. "You know what I mean."

"I thought you wanted me to stay away from the Pride."

He twisted the lid and set the pouch on the ground. "I think you should embrace whatever life Callie Wendell wants to live, and I think time apart from the Pride will help you figure out exactly what that is. Their influence is too strong when you're with them day in and day out."

"I have so much power, Nathaniel. So much to offer the world."

"You're under no obligation to act, Callie. You didn't ask for magical enhancements. They were forced upon you when you were too young to have a voice."

"But have them I do—so what now? I sit back and watch

the world burn because I resent what happened to me?" I felt conflicted. No surprise there.

Nathaniel patted my knee. "Give yourself time. You only just learned who you really are. Once that news settles, everything else will fall into place."

"I don't remember you being this relaxed about things when I was younger. Is that because I was fragile?"

He laughed so hard that it evolved into a snort. "Fragile like a bomb, maybe."

"Sleep well," I said. I squished the pillow to get the filling the way I liked it.

I listened quietly to Nathaniel's even breaths and thought about the Sunstone. Now that it was safely back at Pandora's Pride headquarters, the inner circle would be free to use it to make more of...me. I'd never forgive myself if other innocent children were turned into monsters. I didn't choose to have fangs and wings and magic—the powers of all five species. No wonder my father had stolen the Sunstone when he'd kidnapped me. He'd hidden us both because he couldn't risk letting either one of us fall in anyone's hands. As far as he was concerned, everyone's hands were the wrong ones. I was inclined to agree with him.

I returned my head to the pillow and closed my eyes. Thoughts of Saxon immediately pressed forward. Tonight I lacked the strength to fight them. I pictured his strong jaw and powerful build. His dark wings. The feel of his arms around me and inhaled his scent. Although he was half angel, he didn't possess the ability to dream walk, therefore, any communication would be up to me. I'd resisted so far, mostly because I didn't know what I wanted to say. I wasn't ready to reveal everything I'd learned. I was curious to know what he'd been told by Abra and the others, though—whether she'd try to turn my friends against me. The witch had proven she'd go to great lengths to get what she wanted and right now she wanted me.

I curled into a tight ball, opting for a defensive position as I slept. It was time to face my fears. Ever since I discovered the truth from Abra, there was a part of me that wondered whether Saxon knew. He'd *seemed* shocked to learn that Doran had been eavesdropping on our dreams. What if it was an act? What if all of Saxon's behavior had been an act? He was, after all, the team leader. The one the elders depended on to follow orders and run a tight ship. If there was a chance Saxon knew the truth, I wanted to hear it straight from the hybrid's mouth.

I felt like I was moving in slow motion and opened my eyes. I sat in a cramped carriage with a view of the ocean.

The Ferris wheel on the boardwalk.

I twisted to look at Atlantica City behind me. Darkness had settled over the town and the casinos were lit like beacons in the night. When I turned back to the ocean, Saxon was across from me.

"Is it really you?" he asked. His face looked worn, as though he hadn't rested in days. His wings were barely visible, tucked behind him like a cushion.

I fought the urge to leap across the gap and embrace him. "It's me."

"I've been waiting for you. Every night." He shook his head. "Why haven't you come?"

"Why do you think? So Doran can spy on us and report back to the inner circle?"

He glanced away. "I'm sorry about that. If I'd known, I would've stopped it."

"You swear you didn't know?"

His head jerked to attention. "Are you seriously asking me that?"

"I need to hear it from you."

"No," he said heatedly. "And it will never happen again. It was a violation, Callie. I felt sick afterward."

I nodded. So had I.

"Is that why you left? Why you didn't get in touch?"

"It's not the only reason."

We stared at each other for a long moment as the Ferris wheel inched its way around. As we hovered at the apex, my stomach dipped. I wanted to reach for him. To scrap the whole horrible conversation and just hold him.

But I couldn't. There was too much at stake.

"Talk to me," he urged. "I know something happened, but no one's telling us anything. Tate tried a listening spell. Even Liam wormed his way into a vent…" He trailed off. "It doesn't matter."

"It matters," I said firmly. "Thank you for sharing that." It meant a lot to me that they cared. Before I went to Atlantica City, I could count on one hand the number of others who cared about me. Pandora's Pride changed that. I could use both hands now.

His mismatched eyes met mine. One blue. One green. Both beautiful. "Tell me why you left. Please."

"Has Abra said anything at all?"

"She's been avoiding us as much as possible. The new healer, Renee, has been giving Doran a tonic to help him sleep. Liam reported that one after he accidentally overheard their conversation. Purvis has been in a bad mood. Natasha has been on more of a rampage than usual. We're all staying out of her way. Whatever it is, I know it's big."

"Oh, yeah. It's big." That was an understatement.

He leaned forward and clasped my hands in his. "I miss you, Callie."

Tears pricked the backs of my eyes. "I miss you, too." The rough texture of his hands felt so real, it was as though I was actually with him.

"Tell me," he whispered.

"The elders have been keeping secrets from you. From all of us. They're not the kind of supernaturals you think they are." And neither was I.

"What kind of secrets?" he asked. His face radiated with curiosity and concern. He didn't know. He couldn't.

Yet how could he not? He'd been raised there. They were a smart group. Did they never ask questions about their backgrounds? Maybe they did and their questions were answered with lies. What reason would the children have had to disbelieve them?

"They don't care about us," I said. "We're nothing but disposable foot soldiers."

He squinted at me. "What makes you say that? They care if someone is trying to hurt us. Look at the Order of Beltane."

"They care about their secrets more."

"You're being too vague. I need more."

I returned my gaze to the black water of the ocean. I found no comfort in the sound of the waves tonight.

He released my hands and leaned back. "You're complaining about their secrets, but you get to keep yours? Do you not see the irony?"

My head swiveled back to him. "They basically brainwashed you."

"Callie, no one has brainwashed me. I might work for them, but I'm capable of independent thought and action." Gingerly, he tapped my foot with his. "If I were some kind of puppet, don't you think I would've told them about your fangs."

"Maybe you did. How can I be sure?"

"I swear, I wouldn't do that to you." His expression turned solemn. "Don't you trust me anymore?"

My body felt like it being torn in two. I wanted to believe him. To trust him. I was so confused.

I observed the rides around us as we rolled closer to the boardwalk.

"Come back," he urged. "Not in a dream. In real life."

"I can't."

"You can. You just won't."

"We can't do this." I gestured between us. "Even if I were to come back, this relationship is forbidden."

"I'd still rather have you with me than far away. I don't want to worry about you. Those fae warriors aren't going away and you're leaving yourself vulnerable."

I leaned my head against the side of the carriage. "I don't know, Saxon." There was so much more I wanted to tell him, but I couldn't bring myself to say the words. The revelations were too weighty.

"We're stronger together than apart," he said. "Everyone considers you one of the team."

"Evadne doesn't care if I leave."

He grunted. "And nobody cares if Evadne leaves, but she's still there." He broke into a grin. "You have to learn to ignore Evadne. That's how we've learned to tolerate her."

I nudged him with my foot. "You've had years of practice."

"I hate to think this is the only way we'll be able to meet from now on," he murmured. "Not much of a future in it."

I didn't have the heart to tell him that neither of us might have much of a future at all.

The carriage arrived at the base of the Ferris wheel and the side door swung open.

"That's my cue," I said, standing to leave.

He grabbed my hand. "Don't go. Stay a little longer."

I squeezed his hand and released it. "Talk to Abra. They're her secrets to spill. I don't want the burden." Nor did I deserve it.

"I'll be here whenever you want to come back," he said. "You can count on me."

I lingered for a moment outside the carriage. His eyes burned with desire and I felt every flicker of his raging inferno, but I couldn't let it consume me. I had other priorities now.

My stomach clenched as desperation clawed at me from the inside. I didn't want to leave without kissing him one last time.

But I did.

CHAPTER THREE

THE EVENING MEAL was a coven-wide affair. Long wooden tables were set up outside and fairy lights were strung along the tree branches overhead. The air was crisp and cool but no one seemed to mind the chill. When a plate laden with food was set before me, I forgot all about the temperature too.

"I love each and every one of you," I said, salivating at the sight of drumsticks, corn on the cob, and a poppy seed muffin.

A witch across from me slid a bowl toward me. "Mashed potatoes," she said.

"Oh, thanks, but I can't. I'm lactose intolerant," I said. I sure wanted to, though. They looked delicious.

"Wine?" another witch offered. She pushed the pitcher over so I could reach it.

I poured the wine into a goblet and flicked a guilty glance in the direction of the gate.

"Can't you make an exception for Nathaniel?" I asked. "The poor guy has been looking after me my whole life and now he can't even share a table with me."

"I'm afraid it isn't possible," Marie said.

"It's possible," I said. "You just don't want to bend the rules."

Marie pressed her lips together and I couldn't decide whether she was amused or annoyed by my persistence. "We will not change simply because you wish it."

"And that pretty much sums up your attitude to everything." I immediately regretted my response. Marie had taken me in and listened to me. Believed me. I owed her more respect than that.

"I can sense an apology coming," Marie said. "You needn't bother. You speak from the heart, Callie. I understand that. I was similar until I no longer had the luxury."

"What do you mean?"

Her smile turned grim. "When you lead, your priorities shift. The heart must be balanced with the head."

"To be fair, it should probably be that way whether you lead or not."

Marie spooned potatoes onto her plate. "The older I become, the less certain I am about that."

The rest of the dinner conversation was more pleasant and I learned more about the families inside the village. As with many cultures, there was a hierarchy and Salem was the place to be among coven members. There were other villages similar to this one scattered throughout the Berkshires, but none as coveted as this one.

"You may make use of the guest cottage tonight," Marie said, after we'd finished apple crumble for dessert.

"That sounds luxurious," I said.

She smiled. "It has a bed and a place to wash."

"Like I said, luxurious." I glanced at Marie. "You know indoor plumbing is a thing, right? And electricity."

"Those are things that would force a connection with the outside world," Marie said. "Our simplicity allows us to remain self-sustaining. Our way of life limits our exposure to others."

"And you send Amity in for the daily trip into town for necessities." I made a show of dusting off my hands. "Everything's sorted."

"We're perfectly content," Marie said. "There are fresh towels and soap inside. Let us know if you need anything else."

"Coffee machine? Room service?" I missed Salt with its many bars and restaurants. I even missed the boardwalk with its palm readers and massage parlors.

I missed Saxon and my friends.

Marie patted me on the shoulder. "Sleep well, Callie. See you in the morning."

I tried not to think about Nathaniel as I crept under the warmth of the blankets. He'd survived much worse conditions. Snowstorms. Avalanches. A chilly autumn evening in Salem, Massachusetts was nothing to him.

I kept my head clear as I closed my eyes and prepared for sleep. I didn't want to dream walk tonight. I wanted rest, pure and simple. My body needed it and so did my mind.

So did my heart.

Tomorrow I'd talk to Marie about magic. I was curious about Abra's magic and the powers I might have 'inherited.' Abra had never been particularly forthcoming about her abilities. I knew she could transform into a bird because I'd seen her, but she didn't educate me in the same way as the others. Lloyd was the one I'd turned to for witch-related magic. The wizard was an excellent teacher; it helped that he lacked Abra's withering stare.

I awoke the next morning feeling refreshed and ready to tackle the day. A steaming bowl of porridge laced with honey was waiting on my doorstep. A handwritten note beside it read—*made with oat milk.*

"Wow. Take that, Oren. There's room service here after all."

I carried the bowl to the small table and ate like I might never eat again. I even licked both sides of the spoon for good measure. I had to admit, there was something cozy and appealing about coven life in Salem. It wasn't that far removed from my upbringing. In fact, I'd argue it was a step up, but I missed the accoutrements of life in Atlantica City—and the companionship, of course. I wondered whether the team had a new assignment and how they'd fare without me. They'd managed to fight demons for years before I came along. No doubt they'd be fine.

I brushed my teeth and savored the minty goodness before heading outside to find Marie. She was easy to spot, offering instructions to two younger witches learning to tend to the herb garden. I thought of Abra in her beloved greenhouse. Must be a family trait.

"Sleep well?" Marie asked.

"Yes, thanks."

"What are your plans for the day?"

"I was hoping we could discuss magic together," I said. "I'd like to learn more about my capabilities."

At that moment, Helena rushed forward, tripping over a tree root in her haste. Her cheeks were flushed and her eyes wide with fear. She pulled herself to her feet without bothering to brush off.

"Excuse me, Marie, but there are men with weapons outside the gate."

Marie's body stiffened. "Warriors here?"

"I believe they are fae," Helena said.

Marie didn't waste time asking questions. She raced to the gate where a group of witches had already gathered.

I peered through the slats to see a row of fae dressed for

the battlefield. My heart sank at the sight of the Order of Beltane.

Terrific.

"I know them," I said quietly.

Marie's jerked toward me. "You brought these creatures to our doorstep?"

"I don't know how they tracked me here," I said. "They're called the Order of Beltane. The most important thing to know about them is they want to kill me." They sought to kill all mixed species because they viewed us as abominations. "Be careful. They can portal."

"Not in here, they can't," Marie said.

The wall of warriors parted and another fae stepped through the gap with his helmet on and his sword brandished. My pulse sped up when I saw that his blade was pressed against Amity's neck. I looked from left to right, my heart beating rapidly. Where was Nathaniel?

"Let her go," Marie said firmly.

"A trade," the warrior said and I recognized the voice of Naois, a warrior I'd encountered before. "Your witch for the monster."

I felt the eyes of the coven on me. Only Marie knew my secret and I'd intended to keep it that way. Apparently not for very long.

"You are mistaken. There are no monsters here." Marie took a step forward, radiating authority.

"Then your eyes deceive you," Naois said. "Because the creature stands beside you now."

Marie lifted her chin a fraction. "This *creature* is one of us, as is the witch you threaten. Please lower your weapon and leave our land immediately, or we will be forced to take action."

"I'm afraid that won't be possible," the fae said.

There was nothing as awkward as two polite parties

duking it out. It was like watching Jane Austen characters struggle for dominance at the ball. I'd learned to fight with feral vamps and werewolves in the mountains and then with demons as part of Pandora's Pride. This formal approach to smackdowns wasn't in my wheelhouse.

"Then I suppose we are at an impasse," Marie said.

"If someone throws down a handkerchief, I'm going to lose it," I said. I edged in front of Marie. "Naois, let Amity go. She's a sweet witch—pure, just the way you like your supernaturals."

"One sacrifice for the good of many," Naois said, unpersuaded.

"If you harm a hair on her head, it won't be one sacrifice, my friend," I said. "It will be many."

"Come out from behind your mother's skirts," one of the fae sneered. I couldn't tell which one. With their general appearance, they looked far too homogenous to tell them apart—except Naois, of course. But he and I had an unpleasant history.

I stepped closer to the gate. "Why don't we hunt the real monsters? Plague demons are out there and they're destroying the world piece by piece. Why not join forces and fight them together?"

The fae stared at me blankly.

"Do I have something in my teeth?" I ran my tongue over the top of them. "Look, I appreciate that you guys are all kitted out and ready to rumble, but I highly recommend you redirect your energy to a more worthwhile enemy. Tracking me down is a waste of your valuable time."

Naois tightened his grip on Amity. "Enough chatter. Give yourself up and we will leave the witch unharmed."

"If I come out there, Naois, I can promise you that nobody's leaving unharmed." I turned to look at Marie. "This is the part where he huffs and he puffs and threatens to blow the house down."

Marie wasn't amused. She picked up a stick from the ground and began to chant under her breath.

"What are you doing?" I asked. And where was Nathaniel? I couldn't fight these many warriors on my own, but the werewolf and I could make a strong showing. Maybe a few witches would help. One could hope.

The end of the stick began to glow a brilliant orange. Marie continued chanting and I noticed that the other witches also had sticks in their hands. Primitive wands. Interesting.

"This is your final warning," Marie said. "We have no quarrel with you, fae. Our preference is to preserve the peace that has existed between us for all these years."

"You seem to misunderstand which one of us has the upper hand," Naois said. He wiggled his fingers before returning them to the hilt of his sword. "One quick slice of her neck should remind you."

Marie was the first to throw her stick. It wasn't the move I expected and neither did the fae. The magical weapon flew up and over the gate and landed at the feet of the warrior with a faint hissing sound.

Naois glanced down at the glowing stick and laughed. "You missed."

When I looked at the stick again, it was no longer there. A snake had taken its place. More sticks flew over the barrier and landed on the ground in front of the warriors.

The first reptile opened its jaws and sunk its fangs into the fae's leg. Naois wailed and released his hold on Amity long enough for her to slip away. The fae were too busy staving off the snake attack to stop the young witch from returning to the safety of the village. The gate slammed closed behind her and she rushed into Marie's arms. Her cheeks were stained with tears and her body was trembling.

"I'm sorry, Amity," I said.

The young witch said nothing. Her sister joined the reunion and I turned away, the heavy mantle of guilt settling on my shoulders. If something had happened to Amity, it would've been my fault. I couldn't stay here, not anymore.

I watched through the slats as the warriors trampled the last of the snakes. Naois looked pretty steamed about this reversal of fortune.

"Better luck next time, buddy," I called with a wave.

A portal appeared behind them and the fae warriors jumped through the glowing circle one at a time. Naois was last. He turned for one last look at me.

"We shall meet again," he said.

"I look forward to it. Next time bring flowers. I'm partial to lilies."

He scowled and leaped into the portal.

Only when the portal dissipated did the tension leave my body. I closed my eyes and drew a cleansing breath before facing the witches.

"Do you now understand why different species cannot work together the way my sister believes?" Marie asked. "Those fae care nothing for witches. They only want to pursue their own goals."

The arrival of the fae warriors had thwarted whatever headway I might have made with Marie. "Except different groups of supernaturals are already working together with success. Those warriors are extremists. They don't represent all fae." I thought of Emil. The older fae didn't put the interests of his species above all others. He worked for the good of the whole world.

"We have worked hard to distance ourselves from trouble," Marie said. "I can't jeopardize that, not even for you. I'm sorry."

"I was already mentally packing," I said. "They've only left so they can regroup. Now that they know the location, they'll keep coming until they've smoked me out. The only way to avoid that is to leave."

Marie's expression was solemn. "I would have liked more time to know you, but I have to think of the coven."

"And put your interests first, same as the fae. Funny how that works." I smiled in the hope of tempering the rebuke.

"My obligation is to the witches in this village," Marie said.

"Only because you decided it should be. Why not make your obligation to the rest of the world? The coven is still part of that. It's not like you'd be sacrificing them to achieve a greater goal."

Marie gazed at me, her eyes softening. "We'll have to agree to disagree."

"Thank you for letting me in. For accepting me." I didn't realize how much that acceptance truly meant to me until I said the words out loud.

"I'm sorry it took me a week to relent," Marie said. "I squandered the time we could've had before they found you."

I walked to the gate, accompanied by Amity and Helena. "You'll need a little extra magic when you're outside the village, at least for now."

"Are you certain they'll return?" Amity asked.

"Only to look for me. Once they're satisfied I'm gone, they'll leave you alone."

Amity's round eyes met mine. "Why do they wish to harm you?"

"Because I'm different. The kind of different that causes them extreme discomfort."

Helena scrunched her freckled nose, mulling over my words. "Why should discomfort bring them to violence?"

I patted her cheek. "You can trace it back to fear. They fear what they don't understand and what they can't control." I wasn't hurting anybody. Hell, I was putting myself in harm's way to stop demons from hurting lots of anybodies, but that wasn't enough for this fringe group of fae. They wanted their supernatural lines pure and they'd go to extreme measures to keep them that way.

"Stay safe," Amity said. "I hope we meet again."

"Same." The gate opened and I left the magical sanctuary, my boots heavy with regret.

I didn't have to go far to find Nathaniel. The moment I stepped onto the wooded path, he dropped down from a branch and landed nimbly beside me.

"You do that well for an old man."

"Years of practice."

"I know, but I expected a creaky knee to give you away."

He smiled wryly. "My joints are well-oiled."

We continued walking side-by-side.

"Thanks for coming to my aid during that particularly tense standoff," I said.

"I was watching from a safe distance. If all hell had broken loose, I would've been there."

"Did you at least pack up our stuff while I was doing the actual heavy lifting?"

"I've got everything packed and ready to go." He pointed forward.

"We need a new mode of transportation. I don't know how they tracked me here, but we can't leave anything to chance."

Nathaniel nodded somberly. "Already taken care of."

My brow lifted. "You got rid of the motorcycle?"

He shrugged. "Sacrifices had to be made."

"What do we have now?"

"A green minivan."

I looked at him askance. "The kind with the side door that slides across?"

He nodded. "Like I said, sacrifices had to be made."

"I hope Betsy can stand to add a few more miles on the gage."

He cast me a sidelong glance. "Who's Betsy?"

"The minivan. Who else?"

Nathaniel shook his head. "It's a vehicle. An inanimate object. It doesn't need a name."

"Hey, some people used to think you were an inanimate object around the campfire, but we still called you Nathaniel."

"And why do we need to add more miles? Where are we headed now?"

I remembered the angels that Doran had called upon when we were sent to visit the ogres. It was possible they'd have information to share about Doran's history and my celestial abilities.

I smiled at the werewolf. "How do you feel about Florida?"

CHAPTER FOUR

ONE WOULD THINK because I have the ability to create portals that we wouldn't need to drive a minivan down the entire length of the East Coast.

One would be wrong.

Although Nathaniel and I had been engaged in a crash course of Everything You Need to Know about Being Multiple Species, some of the more advanced moves were too shaky to be trusted. If I messed up the portal, I risked sending us somewhere we couldn't easily escape from—like the underworld or Ikea. Evadne hadn't yet mastered portals after years of practice, so I was doubtful I'd surpass her in a matter of weeks. Then again, I was supposedly more powerful and more 'perfect.' No point in setting limits on myself when I could just test them. Nathaniel seemed to think I was an expert, so who was I to doubt him?

It was in a diner somewhere in North Carolina that I was reunited with a friend in the most unexpected of places—the restroom. I'd flushed the toilet and opened the stall door and nearly walked straight through a portal.

"What the hell?" I backed into the stall and slammed the door.

"Callie?"

My heart skipped a beat. "Tate?" Before I could stop them, tears filled my eyes and I ripped open the stall door.

The portal was gone and Tate stood by the sink. Her hair was a little longer but otherwise she looked exactly the same.

"Thank the gods," she breathed.

I wasn't sure what she'd been told about my abrupt departure. I didn't trust Abra to tell the truth, so I was curious to know what had been shared with the team. The fact that Tate was here now suggested they hadn't painted me as enemy number one.

"Can you please come out of the stall so I can hug you? I love you but not that much."

I took a step forward and Tate threw her arms around me. "Of all the diners in all the world…"

Her laughter was muffled against my shoulder. "It's not a coincidence, you nitwit. We tracked you here."

"I tossed my phone. How is everyone able to find me?"

"Everyone?" she asked.

"Okay, maybe an exaggeration. The Order of Beltane."

She gasped. "You fought them alone?"

"Not quite." I didn't want to say any more than necessary. "We have a table. Do you want to join us?"

Tate cocked her head. "Who's us?"

"Nathaniel."

"As in your father's friend Nathaniel? The werewolf?"

"One and the same. Come on. I'll introduce you." I clasped the witch's hand and tugged her back to the booth where a plate of meatloaf awaited me.

"Nathaniel, I'd like you to meet Tate."

The werewolf didn't bat an eye at the sudden appearance

of a witch from Pandora's Pride. "Nice to meet you. Any friend of Callie's is a friend of mine." He bit a hunk of meat off a bone and chewed. "You are friends, aren't you? None of that frenemies business."

"We are." I slid into the booth and left enough room for Tate to join me.

She eyed the food on my plate. "That looks like something Saxon would eat."

I glanced back at the plate and realized she was right. That was probably the reason I ordered it.

"How did you find us?" Nathaniel asked.

"Why are you hiding?" Tate shot back.

"We asked first," I said. I offered her meatloaf on the fork but she declined.

"We did a spell with one of the many things you left behind," Tate said.

"Oren let you into my room?" I asked, visibly annoyed. That vampire would get a piece of my mind if I ever saw him again.

"Define 'we,'" Nathaniel said.

Right. Back to the important details.

"Me, Evadne, and Liam," Tate said.

There was, of course, one name noticeably absent from the list. I couldn't exactly blame him, but it hurt all the same.

"We opened a portal on the roof of Salt," she continued. "The elders don't know."

"Why?" I asked. "What would they say if they knew?"

"They told us to leave you be," Tate said. "So I imagine they won't be happy with us if they find out."

"I take it Evadne is waiting on the roof to open another portal and bring you back," I said.

"Not just me." Tate cut a hopeful glance at me.

A torrent of emotions rushed through me. I felt so torn

about—everything. "I can't go back, Tate. There are things you don't know."

"Then tell me."

"Ask your grandmother."

She looked down at the table. "Something happened and no one will tell us what it is."

"But they told you something," Nathaniel interjected. He was watching Tate intently.

The witch hesitated. "They might have hinted that…No, forget it."

"Hinted what?" I pressed. I wanted to know exactly what the inner circle was telling the rest of the team.

"They hinted that you might try to come back and steal the Sunstone so you could sell it, which of course we don't believe." She turned to face me with a pleading expression. She didn't want me to think for one second that she bought into their 'suggestion.'

"If I took possession of the Sunstone, I'd destroy it."

Tate's mouth dropped open. "Why would you do that?"

I heaved a sigh. "I have my reasons."

Tate turned away from me and buried her face in her hands. "Please, Callie. Tell me what they are because I am so confused right now."

"I can't."

Tate tore a straw wrapper into tiny pieces. "Do us both a favor and be careful. We've heard reports of rogue demons in this region."

Nathaniel snorted. "Aren't all demons rogue?"

I frowned at Tate. "The team isn't coming to deal with them?"

The witch shrugged. "There hasn't been anything concrete. Purvis said there's a werewolf stronghold not too far from here that will alert us to an incident. I'm sure if something pops up on the radar, we'll be there."

And hopefully Nathaniel and I would be long gone by then.

"Stay safe," I said.

She bumped her arm against mine. "The team doesn't seem the same without you."

"You fought together for years before I came along. I'm confident you'll manage."

"I didn't say we couldn't manage. I said the team isn't the same." Her phone buzzed, prompting an extended exhale. "Time's up. The portal is opening in two minutes."

"So soon? At least stay for a piece of pie." I flashed a cheesy smile. "You know you want to."

Reluctantly, she returned to her feet. "Are you coming?"

I shook my head. "I told you I can't."

She licked her lips. "Fine. I'll tell them what you told me."

"You say that like you don't believe me."

Her expression clouded over. "No, I believe you. I just don't know that I trust you anymore."

My chest tightened. "Talk to Abra. Demand the truth."

"I'd rather hear it from you."

I shook my head sadly. "I've told you as much as I think you'd be willing to believe. The rest has to come from them."

"Them? I thought it was Abra."

I fidgeted with the edge of my napkin. "They all know—Natasha, Emil, Purvis, Doran. Ask any one of them. You deserve to know. You all do."

Tate cast an apprehensive glance toward the restroom. Light glowed in the gap beneath the door.

"I need to go. Take care, Callie. We miss you."

"I miss you, too."

I watched her walk away and part of me longed to run after her and rejoin the team. I wanted to laugh at Liam's stupid jokes and roll my eyes at Evadne's bravado. I wanted to run my fingers through Saxon's hair.

I slumped against the seat. "That was unexpected."

Nathaniel gave me a sympathetic look. "For what it's worth, I think you did the right thing."

"The right thing sucks." I picked at the remainder of my meatloaf, but my appetite was officially gone.

CHAPTER FIVE

WE HADN'T DRIVEN VERY FAR from the diner when thunder rolled in the distance. I shot a quizzical glance at the sky, which was currently a soft shade of blue.

"Do you sense anything?"

Nathaniel sniffed the air. "No."

"Neither do I."

Strange. Nathaniel could smell a storm coming from miles away. I'd always had a decent nose, but my skills were on another level now that I no longer drank the Green-Eyed Monster, the inhibitor potion my dad used to give me. Of course, I didn't know it was an inhibitor potion. I thought it was magical medicine to treat a disease it turns out I don't actually have. I understood my father's decision a little better now. He had to do *something* to suppress my variety of abilities or I would've stuck out like a vampire in a wolf pack. No one on the planet was a quint-brid. Okay, I had to come up with a new name because that one wasn't working for me.

We parked the minivan just in time to see a nearby pickup truck lift into the air and land on its side. Glass shattered as the side window made impact with the concrete.

"What the hell?" I said. My gaze was pinned to the area around the truck. I watched for signs of supernatural intervention, but the air was eerily still.

Thunder rumbled again. This time the sound was much closer.

A man emerged from the store and ran toward the truck. He was shouting and I heard at least one curse word fly from his lips.

The wind whipped past us with such force that I felt the car lift gently off the ground before returning with a soft thud. We exchanged looks as we rocked gently back to a parked position.

"Elemental magic?" I asked.

"Could be a lot of things," Nathaniel said. He continued to peer through the windshield. "Could even be a freak storm."

Lightning streaked across the blue sky and I rolled down the window for a better look.

"There's a strange energy. Do you feel it?"

Nathaniel chuckled. "You might want to peek at yourself in the mirror."

I glanced at the side view mirror and laughed. My hair was standing on end. "I'd hate to see what you'd look like in wolf mode right now."

"It's static electricity."

Rain began to fall from the clear blue sky and pummeled the minivan. People outside dove for cover.

"This is more than a freak storm," I said, rolling up the window.

I peered through sheets of torrential rain for a glimpse of the responsible party but saw only moving shadows.

Another car flew into the air and spun around sideways before being tossed across the town square. Thankfully, no one was inside.

Every window along the storefront blew out, causing

fragments of glass to cover the sidewalk. I caught a glimpse of a large, fast-moving shadow as it disappeared between two buildings.

"It's a demon attack," I said. "I bet it's the same demon Tate mentioned."

"I think there's more than one." Nathaniel pointed to the right where another shadow loomed. His eyes narrowed. "I've seen them once before. New Mexico."

"What are they?"

"Gogome demons," Nathaniel said. "Storm spirits."

I rolled my eyes. "Great. Because railing against the weather is so effective under normal circumstances."

Nathaniel looked at me. "You and I are better equipped than most to deal with extreme weather conditions. No reason to think we can't handle them in demon form."

I looked back out the window and sighed. "You make a good point."

The town was already in bad shape. The front of the post office had collapsed from the wind and a few more cars were now upside down. These demons could destroy the whole town in twenty minutes if we didn't stop them.

"What's their end game?" I asked.

"Destruction and chaos, that's pretty much it."

I glanced at him sideways. "No redeeming qualities at all?"

"They're demons, Callie," he said, as though that answered the question. Well, it kind of did.

I rolled my head from one side to the other in an effort to loosen up. "Okay. You're the expert. How do we defeat them?"

"I'm a werewolf. My moves are limited to tearing them to pieces and..." He paused, pretending to think. "Tearing them to pieces."

"No known weaknesses?" Where was Nita when I needed her? Or Tate, for that matter. Tate was good at research, too.

The ground shook as thunder boomed. "I'm guessing some kind of rainbow laser won't help."

Nathaniel shook his head. "Rainbows come after the storm has blown through. They don't defeat the storm."

I cracked my knuckles. "Then I guess I'll have to rely on good, old-fashioned brute force…and magic."

I braced myself for the rain and vacated the minivan. "Stay safe, Betsy," I said.

My fangs elongated and powerful wings fanned out behind me.

"Cover me," Nathaniel said and charged.

He shifted so fast that his body was a blur. How he expected to attack a shadow, I had no idea. I was still wondering that myself.

My hair was matted to my head in about five seconds. Oddly, my wings remained unaffected. I thought the feathers might get weighed down by water, but they were more resilient than I realized.

I launched myself at the first shadow I saw and was pleased to find that it was more solid than it appeared. Part of me worried I'd pass right through it.

I managed to knock the demon backward but it remained upright. Its form vibrated with intense energy and thunder rolled from the silhouette. I wondered whether each demon possessed a specific storm-related power. If that was the case, the thunder demon wasn't going to be as destructive as the wind demon. That one was more than a simple cyclone like the demon that attacked Amity.

As though answering my question, a gale-force wind blew me backward and the strength of my wings was the only thing that stopped me from slamming into the ceremonial cannon in the town square. I hovered in the air, my wings flapping, and observed the demon as it continued its trail of destruction. It seemed the gogome demons were multi-talented like me.

I completely lost track of Nathaniel in the downpour. It would be helpful to know how many demons we were fighting so I could plan accordingly. I'd just have to wing it, no pun intended.

I flew across the town square and turned down an alleyway in search of the shadowy demon. Lightning lit up the air around me and the rain tapered off, momentarily improving my vision.

The shadow rose to the roof of a neighboring building and darted across the top. I quickly followed, unwilling to risk losing sight of it. As I flew, I tried to think of the natural weapons in my arsenal. What good was being a super supernatural if I couldn't even defeat a couple gogome demons?

Lightning flashed again and it hit me—not the lightning. The idea. Photokinesis. I possessed a fae power that allowed me to project and control light. I also possessed the elemental magic of witches. These gogome were basically demonic versions of elemental power. If I could suck all the elemental energy in the air the way Liam sucked all the air out of a room, I'd be golden.

I landed on the rooftop behind the shadow and it turned to face me. There were hints of a pair of eyes but no nose or mouth.

"Hey, friend," I said, wiping the water from my face. "You seem lost. Do you need directions out of town?"

The demon grew larger and I felt the crackling sensation of static electricity building around us.

That's right, pretty lady. Let me have it.

I inhaled through my nostrils and prepared for the onslaught of power. The rooftop shook as the demon unleashed a torrent of energy. Light emanated from it, temporarily blinding me. I kept my feet firmly planted as my body absorbed the light. I opened my eyes and looked at my hands. They crackled with power, as did the rest of me. Even better, I seemed to be radiating a brilliant shade of yellow.

"I am literally golden," I said.

The demon seemed stunned into inertia. I seized the opportunity and flew to wrestle it flat against the rooftop. My body hummed with elemental magic and I worried I might explode.

Which wasn't such a bad idea.

I struggled to keep the demon down. It seemed to require time to regenerate its strength.

I waited until it was almost to the breaking point and then I released the power inside me and channeled it straight into the demon. It crumpled like the Wicked Witch at the end of the *Wizard of Oz*.

"You can give it out, but you can't take it," I said. The schoolyard taunt seemed entirely apt.

Once the shadow dissolved, I abandoned the rooftop and went in search of Nathaniel and the second demon. I hoped the werewolf was okay. He didn't have my abilities and the whole tear-it-to-pieces idea didn't seem optimum now that I knew more about the gogome.

The town was more of a mess now than when I left the square in pursuit of the dead demon. The cannon was sticking out of the windshield of a Hummer. The rain stopped at some point during my rooftop fight, but people seemed smart enough to stay put. There was no sign of anyone outside checking on their car or trying to flee.

I spotted Nathaniel across the square, still in werewolf form. I flew over to join him and prepared for another takedown.

"One down," I said.

The werewolf turned his head and regarded me with

stony silence. There was blood smeared on the side of his coat. He was wounded.

"I can take it from here," I said. "Go back to Betsy."

The werewolf ignored me.

"Seriously, Nathaniel. I can handle this one now that I understand it better. Save your strength. You're going to need it."

The werewolf limped toward the minivan and I scanned the area for the remaining demon. Thunder rolled. A dead giveaway.

I followed the sound to its source. The shadow hovered in front of the fire station. A bright red fire engine sat outside the building and I noticed a half dozen faces pressed against the glass inside the station. They'd wanted to come out and help, but they were trapped inside by the demon.

I had to lure the demon away. If that fire engine flipped up, it could smash right through the station and kill the rescue workers inside.

Lightning flashed and I embraced it. It pricked my skin as my body absorbed the shock and raw power. This demon didn't seem as surprised by my skill set. Its eyes were set slightly further apart than the other demon but lacked the other features as well.

"The pocket realm is starting to look pretty good to you now, I bet. You're thinking you should've stayed behind when the rest of them broke out."

The shadowy figure bolted and I chased after it, relieved when it reached the diamond of a baseball field. No one was at risk of injury here. Once again, I felt the energy building strength within me. The gogome demon pushed a powerful blast of air in my direction and I steeled myself for impact.

The wind didn't knock me off my feet.

I looked at my hands and feet, stable and sturdy. I'd absorbed the wind the same as I'd absorbed the light.

I looked at the demon and smiled.

The gogome tried again with lightning, followed by a mini monsoon. It didn't seem to realize that I was gathering strength with each attempt rather than simply blocking the elements.

As the demon was about to dish out another blast of elemental power, I leaped forward and toppled it to the ground. I pushed out every fraction of light and air and forced it into the demon's depths. Like its friend, the demon couldn't handle the sudden influx of power and imploded.

I stared at home plate, visible now that the demon was gone.

I paused for a moment to make sure there were no other signs of gogome demons. The air had stilled and there was no thunder or lightning. I left the baseball field and jogged back to the minivan. Nathaniel was back in human form and sitting in the driver's seat with the door open. There was a bloody gash on his side but he seemed otherwise intact.

"It'll heal without stitches," he said, before I could open my mouth.

"Can I get you anything? There's a bottle of water in the minivan."

Nathaniel shook his head. "Not anymore. I drank it."

I gaped at him. "While I'm out there kicking demon butt, you're chugging my water supply?"

He inclined his head. "There's a mini mart right here and it's unscathed."

I couldn't say the same for other parts of the town. Those two demons knew how to throw themselves a party.

"The Pride knew about them," I said. "Why weren't they here?"

"Your friend said they would be if an attack appeared on their radar. Maybe this one didn't."

I motioned to the destruction. "Do you seriously think

this didn't get their attention?" I found that impossible to believe. Even if they didn't show up at the beginning of the mayhem, they should have portaled here by now.

"What's the alternative? You call them and let them know your new location?" Nathaniel pressed. "Your friends finding you is one thing. Abra finding you is quite another."

I hadn't let myself consider the outcome of another meeting with Abra. Our last conversation in the greenhouse had been tense but civil.

"I think she's giving me time," I said.

Nathaniel grunted. "To what? Come back and fight for them? She has to know that's never happening."

"I'm her special project, remember? She doesn't want to hurt me."

"Probably because she can't," Nathaniel said. "Have you considered that they might be afraid of you?"

My gaze lowered to the tips of my boots and I took notice of how scuffed they'd become in the past few weeks. "I highly doubt they're afraid." Especially Natasha. The vampire wasn't afraid of anything. Fearlessness sometimes also meant recklessness, but in Natasha's case, it meant perseverance. There was a reasonable chance that vampire would live forever through sheer strength of will.

"Get your water," he said. "We should hit the road. We want to find somewhere to camp before sundown."

I had a feeling he also wanted to put distance between us and the arrival of any Pride members. Tate's visit had been enough.

We ate a quick dinner in a roadside establishment that featured chicken and waffles, which struck me as an odd combination but seemed to be popular in whatever state we were now in.

The weather was cool but dry so we opted to drive off the highway and sleep in the woods.

"If you get too chilly, princess, you can always sleep in the minivan," Nathaniel said.

"Ha! You're hilarious." The temperature was downright balmy compared with night temperatures in the mountains. "I haven't gotten that soft in less than a year."

I tucked myself into the bedroll and prepared for sleep. It was hard not to think about Saxon and the rest of the team, especially after duking it out with two demons. My fighting had improved in the short time since I'd left them, mainly because I was understanding more and more what I was capable of. I knew what fae could do. What witches could do. What angels could do.

What *I* could do.

There was something inherently liberating about embracing your true self.

I curled into a ball and closed my eyes. I was worn out from travel and fighting, but there was something I had to do. The team's absence from the location of the scuffle was gnawing at me. They already knew demons were in the area. They would've been on high alert for any reports and there was no way this one would've escaped their notice.

Yet they didn't show.

If I touched base with Saxon in a dream, I could scratch the itch and sleep peacefully. It was doubtful the elders were monitoring his dreams now. Knowing Doran, he felt too guilty to continue the practice, knowing I was aware of it.

One little peek would be enough to alleviate my concern. I'd seen Tate in person, so it only seemed fair to visit Saxon.

I focused on my breathing and let my thoughts drift to the handsome hybrid. An image of his dark wings danced in my head and a soft smile touched my lips. Now that I was committed to the dream walk, I realized how much I looked forward to seeing him again.

I opened my eyes and saw only darkness. No stars or

moon overhead. No faint lights twinkling in the distance. An abyss.

"Saxon?" Then louder. "Saxon!"

Silence greeted my call. I took a hesitant step forward and then another. I seemed to be...nowhere. I didn't bump into anything or touch anything. I crouched down to place my hands on the earth but felt nothing solid beneath my feet. This made no sense.

My nerves tingled as I continued to survey my surroundings and wait for the darkness to clear.

Nothing happened.

I bolted upright, my body shaking. "Nathaniel!"

The werewolf shot to his feet in the darkness of the woods. "What is it? Where are you?" His head whipped back and forth until his gaze landed on me. "What happened?"

"I don't know, but we have to go back."

He blinked rapidly. "To Boston?"

"No." I climbed out of the bedroll. "To Atlantica City."

CHAPTER SIX

I STOOD outside Pandora's Pride headquarters, unable to breathe due to the lump in my throat. The foyer was in shambles with overturned potted plants and broken glass. I'd immediately dragged Nathaniel back outside to reassess. For all I knew, it wasn't safe to be in there.

"The building was heavily warded," I said. "Practically impenetrable. They couldn't even create their own portals inside. They had to be made outside the building."

Nathaniel picked up a shard of glass and tossed it aside. "Well, something got in. I doubt the Pride made this mess by themselves."

"We need to check all the floors," I said. "Every room."

"Not so fast," a voice said.

I turned to see Kingsley Bryant on the pavement. The vampire looked stylish in a hot pink pantsuit and her signature blond ponytail. Her stiletto heels clicked across the concrete.

"Kingsley, what are you doing here?"

"I live here, remember?"

I shook my head. "I mean at headquarters."

"I have eyes on this building. Their orders were to inform me immediately should someone show up." She smiled, showing her ruby-encrusted fangs. "And someone did. Who's your friend?"

"Nathaniel, this is Kingsley."

He offered his hand but Kingsley recoiled. "Ooh, no. I don't shake werewolf paws."

It was like the supernatural version of cooties.

"Try not to be offended," I whispered.

Nathaniel's hand returned to his side without a word.

"Do you know what happened?" I asked.

"No, but Ingemar and I have vampires working on it."

I balked. "You and Ingemar are working together?" That was shocking news. Kingsley ruled over the Opulentia family and Ingemar ruled over the Potestas and never the twain shall meet.

"Can you blame us? This happened on our territory. If something was powerful enough to take down all of Pandora's Pride, we need to know what it is."

Unease crept through me. I knew something was wrong when I couldn't reach Saxon in a dream, but I didn't expect *this*.

"What do you know so far?"

Kingsley examined her lemon-yellow nails. "There was an eyewitness…"

My heart jumped. "I need to speak to them."

"Hold your unicorn horn there, princess. Ingemar and I both questioned him and he told us everything he saw. Some chick and her minions dragged our friends out of here."

I pressed my lips together in an effort to exercise patience. "I appreciate your interpretation of events, but I want to speak to him myself."

The vampire rolled her heavily-lined eyes. "Fine. You'll

have to talk to Ingemar. The witness is one of his. Joren or something."

"Joren?" I didn't recall anyone by that name. Then again, Ingemar had a lot of vampires on the payroll.

She snapped her fingers. "You know him. Ingemar's right hand in the casino. Creepy guy with the fancy suits."

"You mean Oren?"

She broke into a bright smile. "That's him."

Oren witnessed this? That was great news because the vampire was fastidious. If there were details to be remembered, Oren was the witness you wanted.

"Are you going to look around now?" Kingsley asked.

I glanced back at the building. "Yes."

"Then I want to look, too. I need to know what happened to Natasha."

I nodded. The vampires had been involved in an intimate relationship that ended before my initial arrival in town. There were accusations of cheating and other relationship-enders, but I knew they still cared about each other, as much as I thought either one of them was capable of caring about anything.

"Do me a favor," I said. "Call Ingemar first and have him send Oren over. I'd like to talk to him while we look around." Plus if anything jumped out to grab us while we searched the building, I'd have a few more supernaturals with me. There was safety in numbers; I'd learned that from working with the team.

"No problem." Kingsley pulled out her phone and tapped the screen. "I even put his real name in my contacts."

I frowned. "You didn't have him listed as Ingemar?"

"No, his number was under 'Piss Off.'"

I shook my head. How Kingsley managed to retain control of a major vampire crime family would've been beyond me if I hadn't glimpsed her vicious side on more than one occasion.

I performed a more comprehensive search of the main floor while we waited for Oren to arrive. The vampires couldn't enter the building without me so I stayed close to the escalator and waited for Kingsley's signal. In the meantime, I sent Nathaniel ahead to start combing the other floors for evidence or—I hated to even think the word —survivors.

I heard my name and traveled down the escalator to the entrance. Oren stood outside the door with Ingemar beside him.

"My old pal, Oren," I said.

The vampire bowed his head. "A pleasure to see you again, Miss Wendell."

I shifted my gaze to Ingemar. "You came, too?"

"I didn't want to miss the opportunity to see the inside of this mysterious stronghold," Ingemar said.

For a brief moment, I wondered whether it was a mistake to invite the vampires in, but this was clearly an emergency and I needed their help. Besides, the wards were still intact which indicated that any treasures or weapons would still be locked up or sealed away.

"I'll take the top two floors," Kingsley said.

Ingemar's brow lifted. "You insist on the penthouse even during a search-and-rescue?"

Kingsley tightened her ponytail. "We don't know what we're walking into."

Ingemar gazed at her with amusement. "If you're that concerned, perhaps you should have a few of your employees with you."

"I'm not *concerned*," she said haughtily. "I'm just bracing myself for the worst. If I find Natasha…"

"You won't," I insisted.

Kingsley eyed me. "How can you be sure? Oren didn't see who went through the portal."

My jaw practically unhinged. "There was a portal?"

Kingsley nudged the well-dressed vampire. "Tell her."

I crooked a finger. "Oren, you're with me. You can tell me everything while we scour the building."

As I gained access to the entrance again, I felt relieved that Abra hadn't locked me out. She must not have expected me to make a surprise return. After all, I'd already taken away the one thing that mattered most to them, aside from the Sunstone.

Me.

We rode up the escalator and I alerted them to Nathaniel's presence. "So keep your fangs on a tight leash if you run into a strange werewolf. He's with me."

Kingsley pressed the button for the elevator and we all piled inside. Oren, Ingemar, and I got off on the next floor and Kingsley continued up. I figured I'd start with the training rooms because there'd be less to focus on in the large airy spaces while Oren recounted the story.

Training Room A was perfectly intact. Nothing broken or in shambles. The only thing amiss was a discarded water bottle on the mat. I picked it up and sniffed the lid.

"Liam's."

Oren and Ingemar exchanged curious glances.

"I want to hear everything," I said. "From the number of clouds in the sky to the color of each car parked on the block. Don't leave out a single detail."

"I saw the portal first." He scanned the area around him as though visualizing the pavement outside. "It formed directly in front of the entrance."

"Did someone form it here or somewhere else?"

"I'm not sure," Oren said. He noticed the balcony carved into the far wall. "What is that for?"

"A viewing area," I said. "So Purvis can tell us everything we're doing wrong during training. Stay focused."

We left the room and headed down the hall to Training Room B.

"It might've been formed here. I saw a woman..."

I grabbed his arm. "A woman at the portal? What did she look like? Please tell me you noticed."

Oren's lips parted and I glimpsed a hint of fang. "She was a woman. How could I not?"

Creepers gonna creep.

"She was average height with medium-blond hair cut shoulder-length in a style that was more popular two years ago." The vampire wrinkled his nose. "And she wore sensible shoes."

"What about her clothes?"

"I couldn't see them underneath the white lab coat."

White lab coat? He might've led with that. "Like a scientist?" I asked.

"No, like a doctor."

I frowned. The description sounded like Renee, the new healer.

The new *fae* healer.

My head began to spin and I threw a hand on Oren's shoulder to steady myself. Whatever happened, Renee was involved. An inside job.

"What else did you see?" I asked.

"The dark wings of your friend." Oren glanced at me quickly before looking away. "The hybrid."

"You saw Saxon? Was he okay?"

"I believe he was unconscious," Oren said.

"How did he get to the portal if he was unconscious?"

"He was carried by a team of small creatures," Oren said.

"We've tried to identify them, but our efforts have been unsuccessful thus far," Ingemar interjected. "We even had a sketch artist draw them based on Oren's description. You're welcome to the drawings if you think they'd be helpful."

"Yes, please." I wasn't sure if I'd figure it out without the team, but I had to try. "Why were you here?"

Two creases rippled across Oren's normally smooth brow. "What do you mean?"

"I mean what business did you have at Pandora's Pride headquarters? There's no reason to be in this vicinity unless you're coming here."

Oren's gaze flicked to Ingemar. "I often take walks around town during my break. Fresh air clears the head as well as the lungs."

"Fresh air clears nothing in you," I said. "You're a vampire."

"This block has been part of my regular routine," he said indignantly.

"For how long?" The Oren I knew spent his breaks getting the diamonds in his fangs buffed and mani pedis in the Salt spa.

Ingemar cast a sidelong glance at his right hand. "You know, I was so taken aback by the news that it didn't occur to me to ask why you were in this vicinity."

"I was simply curious to see whether you'd returned," Oren said, his gaze fixed on me. "The guards were tasked with watching for you at the casinos, so I thought I would handle this building on my own."

My face softened. "You were here and witnessed this whole debacle because you were looking out for me?"

The vampire shifted his weight from one foot to another. "Your departure was rather abrupt. I thought it best to monitor the area in case of any unexpected issues."

Oren might be a creepy stalker, but he was my creepy stalker and I'd never appreciated him more.

"I'll be back in a minute," I said. "I want to poke around

Renee's office and see if she left anything behind that might tell us why she's a lying, backstabbing traitor." It was possible that she'd left clues behind that we'd all missed because we had no reason to distrust her.

"Don't hold back, Miss Wendell," Oren said, smirking. "If you have feelings about the fae healer, it's healthier to express them."

As I hurried to the healer's office, I tried not to get my hopes up. If she was smart enough to carry out a plan of this scale, she was smart enough not to leave pertinent information in plain sight. Then again, their departure may not have been as straightforward as she'd planned. If she'd been forced to act before she was ready...

The office was disappointingly neat and tidy. Then again, it was always neat and tidy, even when the space belonged to Harmony. I opened drawers and scanned every inch of paper on the desk for clues. I picked up a framed photo of Renee and a younger version of Renee. The young fae had to be her daughter, yet Renee hadn't mentioned her that I was aware of. Come to think of it, the healer never shared any personal tidbits about herself. Was there a Mr. Renee? It didn't seem likely or he'd be in a framed photo, too. An unpleasant thought snaked its way into my head. What if Renee's daughter was dead? Maybe that was the reason the healer hadn't mentioned her. As much as I disliked Renee, the idea of losing a loved one hit too close to home.

I returned the frame to its original position, although it seemed like a pointless gesture. Renee wouldn't be coming back to this office. Ever.

I continued my sweep of the office, checking the exam room next. A stack of files had spilled from a table onto the floor and I noticed Evadne's name on the top file. I crouched down to examine the files more closely. Saxon. Tate. Emil. Everyone's file seemed to be here. But why?

I dug Abra's file from the bottom of the pile and flipped it open. It shouldn't have surprised me to see that the founding members had files as well. After all, they needed checkups just like the rest of us.

The top page of Abra's file included a list of recent stats like height and weight. Blood pressure. Nothing remarkable. I flipped back a few pages to see whether there was anything noteworthy. The pages were out of order and I had a feeling Renee had spent time rooting through each file during her brief tenure. There was a good chance she used information in their files against them. After all, she managed to remove some of the most powerful supernaturals in the world from their stronghold. That kind of feat required skill and planning.

It also required a reason.

Why would a random fae want to kidnap the members of Pandora's Pride?

"Come to this conference room," Ingemar said, once I returned to the main floor.

I followed the vampire to the room and halted in the doorway. Chairs were overturned and glasses had tipped over and spilled onto the floor.

Ingemar picked up one of the glasses and sniffed it. "Whatever it was, it wasn't plain water."

Renee *drugged* them? She wouldn't have been able to use the same sedative on everyone. The effects would be different dependent on the species. Then again, Renee would know that as a healer with access to their files.

By the time I exited the conference room, my head was spinning with thoughts—not one of them helpful.

"Come back to Salt and rest," Ingemar urged. "Sometimes it's only when we relax that our minds can once again function properly."

Reluctantly, I returned to Salt where I was greeted by

handshakes and warm slaps on the back from the security guards.

"You'd think I've been gone for a year," I said, as I stepped into the elevator that led to Ingemar's office. I'd convinced him to let me look at the sketch before I went to my room. I wouldn't be able to rest otherwise.

"You must understand, Calandra," Ingemar said. "We see the same type of clientele here day in and day out. You were…"

"Different?" I offered.

Ingemar looked at me. "Yes."

"Yeah, that about sums me up." If he only knew the extent of it.

The doors opened and Ingemar was first to exit the elevator. I was eager to get my hands on the drawings and see whether the creatures were ones I'd seen before.

"I can't believe you're voluntarily working with Kingsley," I said.

We greeted Ingemar's secretary as we entered his private office.

"Surely you can understand my reasons," Ingemar said. "If someone is strong enough to take down Pandora's Pride on our own territory, then we have a serious problem."

I smiled to myself. "We're stronger together."

Ingemar sat in the chair behind his austere desk. "And that's amusing why?"

I dropped into one of the chairs opposite him. "Nothing. Forget it."

As angry as I was with the Pride's inner circle, I couldn't imagine the challenges they'd faced when they expressed the desire to band together with other species to fight the Plague demons. Every group wanted to remain insular, to protect themselves above all else, yet even within species there was discord. Vampire clans. Wolf packs. Witch covens. If they could come up with a reason to draw a line, they grabbed their pencil and set to work. Although my father disagreed with the Pride's methods, I think he must've agreed with the underlying principle of uniting against a common enemy because he taught me acceptance over fear or hatred. On the other hand, maybe he taught me that because he knew who I really was.

What I really was.

I remembered asking my father why we didn't include Plague demons in those we accepted. He explained that the demons served no other than purpose than to destroy. They placed no value on life and only sought to wreak havoc and cause pain. He said that, if we let them, they'd destroy the world simply because they could. When I asked how we could stop that from happening, he didn't answer. At the time, I thought it was because he didn't have one. Now I viewed the moment differently. It was guilt that forced my father's gaze away. He knew he was looking at a possible solution and yet he'd chosen to protect a single life over many.

"The world is complicated," I said to no one in particular.

Oren snorted. "And you're only figuring this out now?"

"You have to remember—my life was pretty simple until I came here. Take travelers from Point A to Point B. Survive. That was basically it."

Ingemar reached into a drawer and produced a sketch-pad. "Feel free to take them with you."

I accepted the pad and flipped open to the first page. The creature looked like a petite body builder with bulbous eyes, green skin, and—

"Are those scales?" I asked, peering at the image.

"That was part of Oren's description, yes."

"If Renee was going for a Snow White vibe, she sure chose the ugliest dwarfs imaginable."

"I take it the creature is unfamiliar to you," Ingemar said.

"Unfortunately, I don't recognize it." Disappointment washed over me. If Ingemar and I didn't know it, what were the odds I could find someone who did? And if these creatures had managed to avoid detection over the years, how would I root them out now?

"Try not to be discouraged," Ingemar said. "We do have one piece of evidence in our favor."

I met his gaze. "What's that?"

"They've been spotted by Oren, which increases the likelihood they've been spotted by others. They might have managed to stay hidden for thirty years, but they've surfaced now. There's no putting the genie back in the bottle."

I nodded as I returned my gaze to the drawing. "I'll find them." I had to because the alternative wasn't worth contemplating.

"This is when I'd take a photo of it and send it to Nita," I said with a regretful sigh. I hoped the werewolf was okay. Nita's power was her brain and advanced technical skills. I had no idea how she'd fare under intense physical and psychological conditions. She hadn't been trained for that.

"What I would like to know is how some of the most powerful supernaturals in the world were overtaken by a gang of sprites, muscles notwithstanding," Ingemar said. "It doesn't seem likely."

"They're obviously minions," I said.

"Even so, Oren saw no evidence of a greater threat."

I studied the drawings, mulling it over. "Renee could be a minion, too. She could've incapacitated everyone before calling in the goblins."

"She was the new healer, you said?" Ingemar raked a hand through his enviable head of dark hair. "She would've known each member's weakness. Had direct access to them."

"She could've drugged everyone at breakfast with a sedative tailor-made for them," I said. My head started to ache. "I need to know more about Renee. There must be a file on her, too. She would've been vetted."

"Not very well," Oren said.

"No. It's understandable though. They were distracted when Harmony left. They only hired someone else because everyone was tired of Emil acting as the healer. It was probably a rush job." I bit my lip, thinking of the former healer who'd been sympathetic to me. "I wonder if Harmony is still local."

Ingemar picked up the phone. "If she is, I'm sure I can locate her for you."

"I would appreciate the help. Renee's last known address, too, while you're at it."

"Do you think it's possible for this fae to be the mastermind?" Ingemar asked. "What could her motive possibly be?"

"I doubt she's the one who orchestrated whatever this is," I said. "But the more I can find out about her, the closer I might get to the real perpetrator."

"You'll need help, Miss Wendell," Ingemar said. "You're only one woman."

I smiled at the vampire. "Oh, Ingemar. I am so much more than that. You have no idea."

CHAPTER SEVEN

INGEMAR'S SECRETARY called me a few hours later with Renee's last known address, as well as Harmony's. Harmony's place was right in Atlantica City, whereas Renee's address was listed as Wildwood. I decided to start there and work my way back to town. Wildwood was only forty-five miles away, a short flight if I used my wings.

The address was three blocks from the beach on a tree-lined street. The olive-colored house had a front porch as well as a second-floor deck and a coveted two-car garage. Garages were hard to come by in these parts; so were cars for that matter.

I banged on the door and waited. I didn't expect anyone to answer and was shocked when the door jerked open. An overweight man in a white tank top and loose-fitting jeans squinted at me with a sour expression.

"Who are you?"

"Uh, hi. My name's Callie and I'm looking for Renee."

"Who's Renee? Did my ex-wife send you? Tell her my girlfriends are none of her business. That's what divorce means." He started to slam the door and I stuck out my hand to stop him.

"How long have you lived here?" I asked.

"None of your business."

"This is Renee's last known address and I just want to know…"

He yanked the door back so that I pitched forward. I managed to catch myself before I landed on my front across the threshold.

"I don't know any Renee," he said. "I've been renting this place for the past four months. My landlord's name is Dirk and he's not married to a Renee. His husband's name is Grant."

"Okay, thank you for your time." I walked away from the house, pondering the possibilities. Maybe Renee had rented this place right before Mr. Pleasant moved in. I could hunt down the landlord, but I had a feeling that would be a dead end. Renee was smart enough to have covered those tracks. The fae community was small in this area given that it was controlled by vampires. There was a reasonable chance that Renee and Harmony knew each other. I took to the air and flew back to Atlantica City to the home of the former Pride healer.

The squat house was the color of a pale seashell. It had a wide, welcoming front porch and a trail of sand on the steps. It seemed someone had recently come in from the beach. I knocked on the screen door and called Harmony's name.

"Callie?"

I turned to see Harmony on the lawn wrapped in a beach towel. Her hair was wet and matted to her head.

"Hi," I said.

"I was in the outdoor shower. Let me just turn off the water and hang my wetsuit to dry." She hurried to the back of the house and returned a moment later.

"I'm sorry to interrupt," I said.

"It's no problem. I'm glad to see you." She motioned to the porch swing at the far end. "Do you mind if we talk out here? I don't like to go inside when I'm still wet. The floor's too slippery."

I sat on the swing and Harmony leaned her hip against the railing.

"I need to ask you about the fae who took over your role as healer," I said.

Harmony frowned. "Why ask me? I wasn't involved in hiring my replacement."

"I know, but I thought you might know something about her. She's a fae called Renee Gladstone."

Harmony's brow creased. "Renee Gladstone? Are you sure?"

"Yes, why?" Her expression was concerning and I hadn't even told her my reason for asking yet.

"How could they possibly have hired Renee?" Harmony seemed to be talking to herself.

"What do you know about her?"

Harmony tightened the towel around her. "She had a known gambling problem. I can't believe anyone within proximity to a casino would hire her."

"She owed someone money?" Who would be rich and powerful enough to take down the entire organization in one fell swoop?

"That wouldn't surprise me."

How could the inner circle have hired someone in debt? That left her vulnerable to blackmail and other kinds of manipulation.

"Any idea which casinos she frequented?"

Harmony laughed. "With an issue like hers? My guess is all of them."

Well, at least I had connections at every casino in town.

Small mercies. "Thanks, Harmony. It's good to see you again."

The fae inclined her head toward her towel. "I'd hug you, but I don't want to flash you."

"It's okay. I'll imagine you gave me one."

She observed me for a long moment, as though deciding whether to ask any questions. "I hope everyone's okay."

I was relieved not to have to lie. "Me, too."

I left Harmony's house and returned to Salt, bypassing the elevator bank to my room in favor of Ingemar's office. If Renee had a gambling problem, there had to be a record of it.

"Mr. Halpain is unavailable right now," the secretary said.

"Emotionally or professionally?" I asked.

She frowned. "Both?"

I couldn't help but laugh. "Accurate. Please tell him..."

"Send her in, please," Ingemar's voice rang out from the corner office.

I thanked the secretary and entered the office.

"Such a purposeful stride," Ingemar remarked. "You know something."

"And I'd like to know more," I said. "I need you to check your records for Renee Gladstone. Give me everything you've got."

Ingemar arched an eyebrow. "I believe I already located her last known address."

I nodded. "You did, but I need you to check your own records—for the casino. She had a gambling addiction. It's possible she was paying off a debt to someone who needed a fae on the inside of the organization."

"Someone who could create a portal."

"And direct access to the members. Someone they wouldn't suspect." When they fired Harmony, they left themselves vulnerable to a situation like this.

"I'll have it done immediately. Wait here."

73

"Really? I had to wait longer than that for my father's killer."

Ingemar's nostrils flared. "That poker chip was decades old. Renee would be in the current system. Much easier to trace."

I rolled my eyes. "Details, details."

He picked up the phone and passed along instructions to an unnamed recipient. "Would you like something to eat while we wait? You must be famished."

"I could eat," I admitted.

"Name the restaurant of your choice. I'll have the entire menu brought up should you wish it."

I smiled at him. "You don't have to coddle me, Ingemar. A platter of scallops will be just fine."

"To the manor born," he said. "As I recall, your first brush with scallops was with me."

"That's true." My stomach rumbled at the thought of delicious food. "It was love at first bite." I paused. "The scallops, not you."

His mouth twitched with amusement. "I assumed as much."

He ordered food to be delivered and I told him how I fared in my search for Renee.

"Harmony knew about Renee's reputation," I said. "I'm surprised Emil didn't know."

"Or perhaps he didn't care. If she appeared debt-free, he might have relaxed his standards a bit in a pinch."

I'd had a similar thought.

The door opened and his secretary shuffled in. "This envelope arrived for you, sir. It's marked as urgent."

"Thank you," Ingemar said.

I noticed that he waited until she left the office to unseal the envelope. "If you don't trust your secretary, it's time for a new one."

"It isn't that I distrust her," he said, his eyes scanning the paper. "It's that I don't want panic to spread. If anyone else learns about the disappearance of your organization, my life will become much more challenging."

"It's not *my* organization."

He ignored me and handed me the paper. "Renee isn't in our special records. She only shows up as an infrequent visitor."

"Then we need to have Kingsley check hers."

A knock on the door interrupted us and the secretary shuffled in again. "I'm sorry, sir. I tried to stop him, but he insisted on only leaving this with you directly."

"It's fine." Ingemar waved her away. "I was expecting him."

The secretary backed out of the office, scowling at the tall, muscular vampire. His large size aside, he wasn't exactly intimidating in knee-length board shorts and a long-sleeved T-shirt with the image of a wave on the front.

"Miss Bryant asked me to bring you this right away." The vampire dropped an envelope onto the desk.

"Tell her thank you for me," Ingemar said.

The vampire lowered his head and left.

I whipped around to look at Ingemar. "How?"

"I was one step ahead of you. My call was to a shared informant."

I hopped up and down in the seat. "Open it."

Ingemar tore open the envelope and plucked out the contents. I watched as he reviewed the information and hope flared inside me when he smiled.

"Renee. Renee." He clucked his tongue. "You've been a naughty fae."

I snatched the paper from his hands and reviewed it, my eyes widening with each new line. Renee most certainly had a problem.

"How could the Pride not have known about this? They have access to records."

"Not these records," Ingemar said. "Like me, I suspect Kingsley only shares what she deems necessary. The rest we keep to our respective businesses. If we'd known she was under consideration, I'm sure Kingsley would have alerted them, but your organization tends to play their cards close to the chest."

I resisted the urge to laugh. He had no idea.

"Renee owes money to so many names," I said. There were varying amounts but all significant. "How do we narrow them down quickly to the most likely culprits?" Time was of the essence.

Ingemar rested his chin on his knuckles. "That's where Kingsley and I can be of use. No need to involve yourself in this part, Callie. We'll simply divide and conquer."

"And what? Have your vampire goons shake them down for information? Do you really think one of these names is our kidnapper?"

"No. I highly doubt any of these names is our kidnapper."

I frowned. "Then why are we wasting time on this?"

"Because one of these names will likely lead us to our kidnapper."

I felt a deep sense of panic. "But that will take too long. We don't have time to play squeeze the lemon, or whatever it is you do to make lemonade."

His mouth split to show his elegantly shaped fangs. No ostentatious display of wealth there. Ingemar Halpain was too classy for jewel-encrusted fangs.

"Can you suggest a faster method, Callie? If so, I'd love to hear it, I'm always open to fresh ideas."

The speaker phone buzzed. "Your food is here, Mr. Halpain," the secretary said.

"Send them in."

The door opened and a vampire in a chef's smock rolled a cart of food into the office. He uncorked a bottle of red wine and poured two glasses. I didn't object. Alcohol sounded appealing right now.

"There's a name here I believe we should move to the top of the list," Ingemar said. "A known associate of demons."

My head snapped up. "Plague demons?"

"There are two types of demons, Callie. The ones with power and the ones without. I only concern myself with the former. The others are pests to be exterminated."

"Plague demons aren't to be exterminated?"

"On the contrary, they are, but that's never been my role. That's the domain of the Pride."

"Only because they're the only ones willing to take it on. They'd be happy to have more associates, I promise you."

Ingemar sipped his wine and said nothing.

I wolfed down my food too quickly to enjoy it. I was hungrier than I realized.

"I advise you to slow down when you drink the wine or you'll be stumbling out of here."

"Good advice." I needed to be at my best right now, not my drunken worst.

"I'll have my team pay a visit to Willem Dougherty and let you know what they find."

"Can I go with them?" I asked.

"I think it's best if you don't. This is a delicate situation, Callie. I can't let customers think I open my private books to anyone."

"Understood." I gulped down the wine like it was water. I'd have to regret my gluttonous choice later. The Pride was missing—Saxon and my friends were in danger—and I wasn't able to interview the one lead I had.

I stumbled out of the office an hour later, feeling ready to puke. I'd overindulged in every way and now I'd pay the price.

I sent a text to Nathaniel with an update and hoped I didn't include too many errors. Although I'd tried to secure a room at the casino for him, the werewolf had insisted on sleeping outside. At first I thought it was because of the vampire-run casino, but he assured me it was that he preferred the beach to a cramped room, which I understood.

It felt good to be back in my room. I stood at the window and watched the waves roll in. A sense of peace washed over me. I pictured Saxon hovering outside the window, his wings spread wide.

"I'll find you," I said. "I'll find all of you."

I showered and dressed for bed, despite the early hour. I was tired and a little drunk, but I wanted to pursue another angle. If I had to dream walk every night of my life, I'd do it if it meant finding them.

I crawled under the covers and snuggled my head against the pillow, making myself comfortable. I tried to manage my expectations. I'd already tried to locate Saxon and failed. There was no reason to think I'd be successful this time. That being said, the connection would be stronger in Atlantica City. This is where we met and forged a relationship. This is where they lived and were taken from. I closed my eyes, picturing Saxon's rugged jaw and smoldering intensity.

It was going to be a long night.

My body floated. I kept my eyes closed, unwilling to break whatever connection I'd managed to form. I let myself drift to the ground like a feather. When I felt solid earth beneath my feet, I dared to open my eyes.

The good news was that I wasn't blanketed in complete darkness. The bad news was that there was no sign of Saxon.

There was no sign of anything. Cracks in the earth were filled with bubbling liquid the color of a fireball. It was like being in the base of a volcano. No vegetation. No horizon. No signs of life.

Was this Saxon's dream? I wasn't sure yet, but my heart beat with fervent hope. I pressed forward, armed with the knowledge that, no matter what, this wasn't *my* dream. I could feel the 'otherness' of it. I didn't know this place. It wasn't in my memories. Although I'd been fooled by dreams of an unconscious memory before, this dream had a different quality to it.

On the ground beneath my feet, a symbol had been carved into the ground. The grooves were so deep that I would have slipped through the chasm if I weren't paying attention. I spread my wings and took to the air for a better view.

An anvil.

Interesting choice. Someone was either extremely bored or the symbol had a meaning I didn't recognize.

I noticed a cliff in the distance and instinctively moved toward it. My body mingled with the wind and I swept down the cliffside to a series of caves. The landscape appeared to be desolate with no sign of civilization.

I arrived at the mouth of one of the caves and peered into the darkness. A figure slept on the stone floor of the cave and I heard my sharp intake of breath. As I rushed forward, I realized the figure wasn't Saxon. She was older and female.

I edged closer and gasped.

Abra.

The older witch was either asleep or unconscious. She lay on her side with her eyes closed and her hands tucked under her cheek in prayer form. She looked vulnerable and not at all like the formidable witch she was. For a fleeting moment, my anger and resentment melted away and I fought the childlike urge to curl up beside her. I never knew my mother and I didn't have a female authority figure in my life until I arrived at Pandora's Pride. My mother's death wasn't their fault. Of course, the blame for what happened afterward laid entirely at their feet. There was no disputing that. I'd been a baby when the Pride had taken me in and performed their magical experiment. I had no idea what was being done to me and no memory of it either. I thought of the elaborate mark on my back, the one that was created when they funneled their supernatural traits into me. The one that identified me as 'theirs.' My father had gone to great lengths to hide any signs of my identity. The shirts had to cover the mark in length and color. The shock of blond hair that framed my face had to be colored. He devoted years of his life trying to protect me, only to end up murdered for his trouble.

I shoved the thoughts aside and crouched beside Abra. Despite my complicated feelings, I had to help her. I needed to try to wake her. This seemed to be her dream. She should be awake in it.

"Abra," I said. "It's me Callie. I need you to wake up and tell me where you are. Tell me who took you."

The witch didn't stir. I jostled her arm and called her name again. Her eyes slid open and for a split second I rejoiced, until I realized she was still unconscious. Or dead.

In an instant, my surroundings dissolved, replaced by white walls and a window. I spotted the familiar small table and a coffee machine. I was back in my room at Salt.

I collapsed against the pillow, my heartbeat thundering in my ears. I didn't learn much except that Abra was in a cave in a barren wasteland.

It would have to be enough.

CHAPTER EIGHT

It FELT strange to be in Nita's lab and looking through her files without the werewolf in the room with me. If anyone could put together the pieces of this puzzle, it was Nita. Unfortunately, she was currently one of the pieces.

"What are we looking for?" Oren asked.

"Any lava-like landscape. There were caves and a cliff. No bodies of water that I noticed."

Oren's phone buzzed and he glanced at the screen. "Mr. Halpain would like you to know that Willem Dougherty is dead."

"That's unfortunate." Our one concrete lead was dead. "Foul play?"

"His neck was slashed," Oren said. He clicked off his phone.

"Help us, computer," I said. "You're our only hope."

I was pleased to see there was no login required. That's what happens when you operate out of a stronghold; you don't expect anyone to breach it. That being said, I had a feeling access to Abra's files would require a set of deadly trials and a sacrificial ritual.

Oren flicked through a drawer of folders with manicured nails. "Hawaii would be nice. Perhaps they've been taken there."

I turned to peer at him. "They're not on vacation, Oren. They've been kidnapped."

I tapped the keyboard and typed a few search terms. I didn't have extensive computer knowledge or experience given my upbringing, but thankfully I'd picked up a few tidbits during my time here.

Oren cast a glance over my shoulder. "*That's* your search?"

I craned my neck to look at him. "What's wrong with it?"

He shook his head. "You won't find anything quickly using *lava, hot* and *hard to escape.*"

"Those are the salient points," I argued.

He suppressed a laugh.

"Laugh it up, Oren. I'd like to see you survive an avalanche or two."

"We all have our talents, Miss Wendell."

"Damn straight."

He motioned to the computer. "Allow me."

I vacated the chair and the vampire took my place. He typed as elegantly as he performed every other task. If there was a finishing school for vampires, Oren had definitely graduated top of his class.

"Firstly, you're not using the correct search engine. This is the one for the average citizen. You need to use what Nita would use for a deep search like this."

"What would Nita use?" I didn't realize there was more than one option.

He clicked on an icon of a black cloud. "She has a back door into a supernatural-centric search engine. Before the Plague, when humans knew nothing of our existence, supernaturals conducted much of their business off the grid, so to speak. As human computer systems grew more sophisticated, supernatural systems went deeper and darker to elude discovery."

"Why does it still exist then, now that we're out and proud?"

Oren frowned at me and returned his gaze to the screen. "Ah, to be young and ignorant. Those of us who've been around for a long time know how fickle the world can be. Granting humans access to our most coveted information might be to our disadvantage later."

"You think they'll rise against us someday?" I pictured the human travelers I'd escorted across the mountains over the years. Their fear and desperation. Humans couldn't safely drive on a main road between cities. How would they possibly gather the knowledge and ability to return the supernaturals to the shadows?

"There will always be a contingency reminding others about the glory days of humankind. When their territories belonged to them and weren't divided among vampires and witches. They will yearn for a simpler time."

"I yearn for a simpler time, too, but I think they're more worried about Plague demons than us," I said. "Especially when we're the only ones preventing their world domination."

It seemed odd to think of humans as 'they'—as separate and apart from me—now that I knew who I really was. Technically, I was one of them.

"Perhaps now," Oren said. "Give it time." His nails clicked across the keys and I watched the search results load.

"I didn't expect much out of this buddy movie, but you've surprised me, Oren." I patted him on the back. "This could be the start of a beautiful friendship."

He sniffed. "And here I thought we were already friends."

"Who documents all these locations?" There were some places I recognized in the results like Tuat, Ti-yu, and

Kuei-Hui, but there were just as many names I'd never heard of.

"There is no single resource for information," Oren said.

"I'm glad you're here," I said. "I wouldn't have known how to do any of this."

Oren kept his gaze fixed on the results, but I saw the hint of a satisfied smirk in the screen's reflection. The vampire liked to be needed, bless his unholy self.

"Were there no signs of the inhabitants?" he asked. "No deities they worshipped or powers they might possess?"

"Nothing except a giant anvil carved in the ground," I said. "I could've fallen to my death in it."

Oren glanced at me. "An anvil, you say?"

"Maybe they're smiths?"

Oren turned back to the screen and the speed of his typing picked up tempo. He seemed to have an idea. I peered over his shoulder at the results.

"I don't think they're in Tartarus, Oren." Tartarus was a chamber in the Greek underworld where the souls of their most wicked were trapped for eternity. The Pride would need to be dead to even enter the underworld and it wasn't open to all kinds.

"I don't either, but the anvil could be a reference."

"I don't get it."

Oren frowned. "Did your father teach you nothing in the mountains except how to set up *camp*?" He pronounced the word 'camp' with utter disdain. "It was said that Tartarus was so deep in the underworld that an anvil would take nine days to reach it when thrown from the heavens."

"And you think this is relevant because…?"

Oren sniffed. "Because I believe the symbolic anvil you saw was a sign of protest." He paused to look at me. "In the pocket realm."

My heart skipped a beat. "Oh, wow. Oren, you just blew my mind."

"There is, of course, only speculation as to what the pocket realm looks like. Very few details are available except with regard to the area where they broke free. No one has ever dared travel there for fear of being lost forever."

My head began to swim with possibilities. "What better place to hide the Pride? The infrastructure is already there and a Plague demon would know the terrain well, so they'd know exactly where to stash them away." A Plague demon would also have the power to persuade a fae and a team of muscled goblins to do his bidding.

The more I considered the options, the more sense it made. Even though Renee and her cohorts managed to get the Pride out of headquarters, it would be extremely difficult to contain them somewhere in this world. Between them, the Pride had just about every power imaginable. If there was a way out, they would find it. And the best way to mitigate that would be to hold them captive outside this realm in the very place the escaped monsters had been imprisoned.

"Except there's a hole where the Plague demons fought their way out," I said. Although it wasn't an insurmountable obstacle. Abra was unconscious in the dream. If they'd all been rendered incapacitated, they wouldn't be able to find their way to the gaping hole.

"I've heard rumors that dangerous creatures still roam there. It's possible the hole isn't easy to access."

"Or its location known," I added. Just because it was called the pocket realm didn't mean the place was small or easy to navigate.

"You would think a demon that escaped would never wish to go back."

"They would if it was the means to an end," I countered.

85

"Or the demon himself didn't return," Oren said. "You don't see Mr. Halpain here, do you? He sent me."

I smiled. "Don't let your boss hear you compare him to a Plague demon."

"Certainly not."

I continued to follow the line of thought. "Plague demons want to take over the world. If you're a Plague demon, what important step do you need to take to achieve that goal?"

Oren steepled his fingers together. "Yes. I see your point." He swiveled in the chair to face me. "Even if your theory is correct, how do you intend to get to the pocket realm and, more importantly, how do you intend to get everyone out again?"

I nodded toward the screen. "We have the advantage of knowing in advance where we're headed."

The vampire arched an eyebrow. "We?"

"The proverbial 'we.'"

"There is no proverbial 'we,'" he scoffed. "There's only the royal 'we.'"

I crossed my arms and fixed him with dagger eyes. "Will you come with me or not?"

His smile was so unusually genuine, it completely changed the appearance his face. He looked almost boyish. "I thought you'd never ask."

I tapped the top of the computer. "We need every detail we can find about the pocket realm. Once we have the information we need, we'll strip the armory bare."

He regarded me. "How do you intend to transport an entire armory to another realm?"

"I'm more talented than I look."

"We need access to a very powerful portal. With Emil out of the picture...?"

"I've got it covered," I interrupted.

"How? It will take far too long to..."

"I said I have it covered," I snapped.

Oren's eyes widened at my tone. "I didn't mean to question your plan, Miss Wendell."

I blew out a breath. "If we're going to be working closely together, you should at least call me Callie."

"I don't know that I can. I'm trained to be respectful."

"You once cornered me in an elevator and tried to kiss me without my permission. How is that respectful?"

He averted his gaze. "I'm a vampire. I have a predatory nature."

I groaned in disgust. "That's the worst excuse I've heard since 'boys will be boys.'"

"Would you like my assistance or not?"

"I would." Very much. I was smart enough to realize I couldn't do this alone, no matter how powerful I was designed to be.

Oren met my gaze with an earnest expression. "Then we need to trust each other, do we not?"

"I do trust you, Oren." I debated whether to tell him my secret. How could he trust me if he learned the truth some other way?

Nathaniel's appearance in the doorway derailed my plan.

"Find anything?" the werewolf asked.

"I think we have," I said. I updated him on our discovery. "Oren is going to play keyboard warrior and find out as much as he can so we go in armed to the teeth with knowledge as well as weapons."

"Sounds like a good plan." Nathaniel nodded to Oren. "Thank you for your help."

"You can thank my employer," Oren said stiffly. "It is Mr. Halpain who insisted on my participation."

I bit back a smile, knowing perfectly well that Oren had jumped at the chance to help. If Oren wanted to scowl and posture in front of a werewolf, who was I to burst his bubble?

"First I need a physical link to Renee," I said. "I'm going to check her office again and see what I can find." The fae created the portal that transported them, as well as escorted them there. A personal item of hers was my best bet to forge a link to the right location. I remembered the framed photograph on the desk in her office. It wasn't guaranteed to create a strong enough connection, but it was better than nothing.

I returned to her office with fresh eyes. The last time I was here, I didn't know what I was searching for. At least now I had an item in mind.

My gaze darted to the chairs in the waiting area where Saxon and I had sat side-by-side after retrieving the Sunstone. I let the memory of him wash over me and treasured the moment. I'd already been missing him. If anything awful had happened to him while I was gone...I blocked any negative thoughts. It was critical to stay focused on the mission and not let my emotions distract me.

As I headed for the framed photograph on the desk, I spotted the closed door for the restroom. There was a general restroom for patients that included a bathtub and a shower for cleaning off the blood after battle, but there was also a private restroom for the healer. It hadn't been worth looking there before. Now, however, it was my best chance of finding a personal item. I clicked open the door and saw a toothbrush and toothpaste. A box of tissues. A bottle of hand soap and a bottle of lotion, each handmade by a mage on the boardwalk called Lulu. More importantly, there was a hairbrush.

Jackpot.

I snatched the hairbrush from the sink and was pleased to see Renee wasn't very fastidious about cleaning out the bristles. For a double agent, she wasn't very smart, unless she assumed there'd be no one left to track them. I stared at the hairbrush, feeling a surge of guilt. If I had been here, would it have made any difference or would I have been taken along with everyone else?

I clutched the brush to my chest and heaved a sigh. Well, I was here now and that's what mattered. Renee was going to rue the day she set foot in Pandora's Pride headquarters.

I returned to the lab with the hairbrush, as well as personal pieces I'd collected from each members' room or bathroom and shoved into a tote bag I found in Tate's room. I'd considered a backpack I found in Liam's room but quickly abandoned it when I noticed one of the straps was sticky.

"You've been doing some shopping?" Nathaniel asked, as I heaved the bag onto the table.

"I have an idea and Renee was kind enough to leave us a sample of her hair which should allow me to experiment."

Oren's head popped around the side of the computer. "The pocket realm makes for fascinating reading. There were several articles written after the Plague, all analyzing the escape and how it could've been prevented if the gods had included a failsafe or simply chosen to destroy the realm once the demons were trapped there."

"They're gods," I said. "They're too arrogant for a Plan B."

Oren looked downright cheerful. "Now we only need to sweep the armory clean and find a fae powerful enough to portal us there."

I exchanged looks with Nathaniel and drew a deep breath. "In the interest of building a solid foundation with you, there's something you should know."

"I knew it," Oren said, deadpan. "You bathe in the blood of unicorns."

I smiled and nudged his arm. "Oren, you made a funny."

"I am capable of humor on occasion, Miss...Callie."

"We don't need one of the fae to create the portal. I can do it."

Oren started to laugh but stopped when he noticed my expression. "You're serious?"

"As Kingsley at a fashion show."

He shot a quizzical glance at Nathaniel. "How? Mages can't create portals. That's the domain of the fae."

"Drumroll, please." I spread my arms wide. "I'm part fae."

Oren scrutinized me. "You're a hybrid like the others?"

"But wait, there's more." I sucked in a breath. In for a penny, in for a pound. "I'm also part wolf."

He touched the side of his nose. "That explains the keen sense of smell. Then you're a tri-brid like Evadne but without the surly disposition. A step up, I suppose."

I held up a finger. "Wait, there's more." I focused on my fangs first, quickly followed by my wings.

Oren rolled the chair away from me, momentarily stunned. "I don't understand."

"The wings are from my angel side and the fangs are vampire. Come on, Oren. You should at least know that much."

"What are all these 'sides?' Are you a Rubik's Cube?" The vampire inched forward, his gaze riveted to my fangs. "Those are real?"

"They come and go, but they're real. Same as the wings." I flapped them for good measure. "I can produce them at will now. It took some practice, but I got there in the end."

Nathaniel chuckled. "Not without a few mishaps along the way."

"That car window was *not* my fault," I said hotly.

Oren continued to gape at me. "You're telling me that you somehow possess the traits of *five* supernaturals."

"And I was born human," I added unhelpfully.

He glanced at Nathaniel for confirmation and the were-wolf simply shrugged.

"Does Mr. Halpain know?"

"No, but I'll tell him." The secret would be out soon enough. I wasn't going to be able to hide the truth once I got to the pocket dimension. There was too much at stake to suppress the powerful parts of me.

"How?" Oren asked.

"That part will remain confidential," I said. No need to air the Pride's dirty laundry. I didn't want to give the vampires a reason not to help me.

"And you're certain you can do this? Create a portal to the pocket realm?"

"I mean, I won't stake my life on it, but I have confidence I can get us there." I wasn't trying to *create* the realm, I was only trying to access it. If Renee could do it, then I had faith I could too.

"How?"

"I suspect Renee aimed for the weakest entry point." I reached over and flicked the tote bag. "And now I have personal items to connect us to Renee and everyone she abducted." I only hoped it was enough.

Oren blinked. "This is quite a lot to digest."

"Can you multitask?" I asked. "Because we need to get moving."

He nodded. "I suppose we should prepare the troops for battle."

We left the office with a plan in place. Oren returned to Salt to update Ingemar and I went to the armory to choose weapons. I wanted to bring enough to pass them around to the team.

"How are we going to carry them all?" Nathaniel asked. He stood beside me and gave the wall of weapons an appraising look.

"I have this." I tilted my head to a backpack hanging from a peg on the wall.

He chuckled. "You won't even fit a double-sided axe in that bag."

"I will once I've used magic."

The werewolf's face lit up. "Your father's spell."

I smiled. "Mage magic has its uses."

When we lived in the mountains, we often had to carry heavy loads for miles. It was worse when we accompanied travelers because we had to handle their belongings as well. The trek was typically too dangerous to have the humans both walk and carry packs. It also slowed us down, so my father would use a bottomless bag spell to help us transport items. Thanks to his spell, we could fit bedrolls, tents, supplies, and food in a single pack. He'd taught the spell to me, although in secret. He didn't want anyone to know I was capable of magic for reasons I didn't understand at the time but didn't question. I trusted my father.

Trust no one, his final words to me uttered with his dying breath. He truly meant no one.

But I didn't want to live that way.

Yes, Abra had lied. All five elders had lied. Even my father and Nathaniel had lied. I refused to stop trusting others, though. It was impossible to form relationships without it. And I wanted relationships.

I wanted connection.

"If you've got this part under control, I'll raid the snack bar for supplies," Nathaniel said. "Wherever they are, I doubt they're enjoying three square meals a day."

"Good idea. Meet me outside the entrance when you're done."

He nodded once before leaving the armory.

I grabbed the backpack from the peg and sat on the floor to concentrate. It had been easy for my father to convince everyone I was half mage, including me. The main difference between witches and mages was that a mage was basically a lower level witch. The fact that I could do this spell as an adolescent wasn't because I was a talented mage, it was because I possessed all the magic of a powerful witch. Of course, that power had been minimized thanks to my daily potion, but I retained enough magic to perform the bottomless bag spell.

As my hands maneuvered over the bag, imbuing it with magic, a memory of my father took center stage. He sat cross-legged with a backpack on the ground in front of him.

Watch me closely, Lark. Watch how my hands move.

My smaller hands moved awkwardly from side to side instead of around.

No, not like that. Watch again. His voice was patient and kind.

I tried again and he nodded encouragingly.

Now you need to create that mind-body connection. That's the key. You can do all the moves correctly, but if you fail to forge that link with your inner self—your core—it won't mean a thing.

My father had tried to prepare me for so many things without revealing too much. He had known there was a chance I'd come into my powers, that the inhibitor potion might not last forever. He'd wanted me to be able to defend myself. He taught me to fight.

He taught me to survive.

Once the backpack was sorted, I carried both bags outside to the entrance where I'd arranged to meet Ingemar and his crew. I was pleased to see the vampires already assembled, along with Nathaniel.

"Ready when you are," Ingemar said.

I shook my hands and rolled my neck from one side to the other in an attempt to loosen up. I'd been practicing portal creation ever since I learned I was capable of it, but this would involve taking my skillset to the next level.

"You look nervous," Oren said. He reached for my shoulders. "Perhaps a quick massage."

I jerked away from him and gave him the stink-eye. "Boundaries," I said sternly.

Oren slunk back into the crowd and I dumped the contents of the tote bag on the pavement at my feet.

"This all looks very professional," Ingemar said.

I glanced up at the vampire. "Do I detect sarcasm, Mr. Halpain? It might look messy, but it's a very advanced combo locator spell/portal creator." Looking good would have to take a backseat to doing good.

"I wasn't questioning your abilities," Ingemar said. "I trust you."

I looked at the vampire with shining eyes. I didn't know why his vote of confidence meant so much to me, but it did.

"Thank you," I said, and returned my focus to the portal. I concentrated on forging that mind-body connection that I knew would provide the foundation for magic of this magnitude. I pictured Renee funneling my friends through the portal. I aimed to recreate the pathway that the fae took to the pocket realm.

My fingers tingled with magic as I pushed the energy out of me and shaped it into a glowing circle.

Ingemar's dark eyes widened. "You'll have to explain this to me when we have time."

I didn't answer. I needed to maintain my focus as I forged a link with the other side of the portal. The pocket realm didn't feel the same as forging a connection with a place here. There was a strange, hollow quality to it, like anchoring to an abyss.

Once I felt comfortable that the link was solid, I enlarged the portal until it was big enough to accommodate our sizes. My backpack might be bottomless, but I couldn't yet squeeze a square vampire through a round portal.

"Stop right there," Kingsley's voice rang out. "What do you think you're doing?"

I turned around slowly to see rows of solidly-built vampires strapped with weapons. If Kingsley chose to get pissy about territory or some equally selfish complaint, she was going to find the stiletto heel of her shoe sticking out of her chest. I didn't care how many witnesses there were.

"What does it look like?" I asked. "I'm creating a portal for our search-and-rescue mission."

"Without us?" Kingsley strode to the front of the line wearing thigh-high boots and a combat vest. "I don't think so, sweetie."

"Excuse me?" I glanced at Ingemar, uncertain. "I thought…I didn't think you were coming."

"You're heading into another realm to take on an opponent so powerful that they kidnapped the entire Pandora's Pride team," Kingsley said. "Do you really think I'd let you do that without the help of the Opulentia family? You need us like I need a watermelon margarita after a tough day at the office."

The vampire closed the gap between us, only stopping when the tips of our shoes were practically kissing.

"You can't come with us and leave your territory vulnerable," I said. "Someone might seize the opportunity."

Kingsley's fake lashes fluttered. "Do you seriously think I've held on to power this long without thinking through the consequences?"

No, I didn't think that for a second. Kingsley was as smart and ruthless as she was beautiful. She was also taking an unnecessary personal risk by joining the rescue party, which wasn't like her at all.

"You want to save Natasha," I said, quietly enough so that only Kingsley could hear me.

Her chin jutted. "Nobody comes onto my turf and steals my woman out from under me. Is your portal ready or what?"

I shot a quick glance at the glowing portal. My portal.

"It's ready."

She let loose a shrill whistle. "Let's go, boys."

The vampires marched forward and stepped through the portal one-by-one.

Ingemar watched them with an expression bordering on annoyance. "Oren," he said, handing his phone to the vampire. "Rally the troops."

I looked at the cluster of vampires standing behind Ingemar. "I thought these were the troops."

Ingemar sniffed. "Apparently not. It seems we need a few more in order to fulfill our obligation to the Pride."

I wasn't about to argue. "The more, the merrier."

Oren's lips parted as he whipped out his phone. "With pleasure, sir."

CHAPTER NINE

THE POCKET REALM appeared as lifeless and desolate as it did in my dream. Ruddy grey stones and a landscape so dry that my lips cracked just looking at it. It was hard to imagine living here for centuries. Then again, Plague demons weren't civilization builders.

They were destroyers.

"Not the ideal vacation spot, is it?" Oren asked, dusting off his crisp sleeves.

"It was created as a prison world, so I wasn't expecting puppies and rainbows," I said.

Kingsley took a few steps forward. "I would kill for some puppies right now."

A few of her foot soldiers took a step backward, appearing to take her words seriously. I had to imagine you lived in fear if you served Kingsley Bryant.

"No guards on patrol, I see," Oren said.

"I doubt they'll have any except the ones keeping the Pride contained," I said. "Whoever is responsible for this has no reason to believe anyone will know where they are or how to come after them." As far as Renee knew, I was never coming back and I was the only one left with the ability to enter Pride headquarters.

Kingsley surveyed the landscape. "The gods sure knew what they were doing. This place is the pits."

"A literal pit," Oren added.

"Emil is adept at portals," Ingemar said. "Why do you suppose he hasn't found a way out of here?"

I thought of the files in Renee's office. "I suspect they disabled Emil and Evadne's powers somehow. Renee seemed to be pretty thorough in her preparations."

The air around us shifted and I suddenly felt overheated. Looking at the others, I realized that Nathaniel and I seemed to be the only ones experiencing a temperature change. It was a good day to be a vampire.

"Why are your cheeks so red?" Kingsley asked. "You look like you overdid it with the blush brush."

"Something's coming," I said.

"I thought you said no guards," she snapped.

"They're probably not guards. They might just live here." The realm might be a good option for lesser demons, now that the main demons had evacuated. They would've moved right up the pecking order.

Oren's gaze was riveted to the horizon. Based on his terrified expression, I was almost afraid to look. I turned slowly and saw what appeared to be a wall of flames moving toward us with purpose. I'd never seen anything like them. As they moved closer, I could see the flames weren't one giant wall but three distinct figures.

"No weapons," I called. "The metal will only melt when it makes contact."

"Vampires don't do well with fire," Kingsley said. "We burn and I just had a facial." She patted her cheeks for good measure.

"These are flame giants," Nathaniel said.

I cut a glance at him. "And I suppose you fought these in New Mexico, too?"

"Arizona," he said.

I shook my head. "How did you have this entire life before you met me?"

He cracked a smile. "Easy. I was born earlier."

Kingsley spit out a wad of pink bubblegum. "How do we kill them, genius?"

"We had a shaman with us who found depriving them of oxygen was the fastest way to beat them," Nathaniel said.

"How?" one of Kingsley's sidekicks asked. "It's not like I can get my hands around its throat without losing my skin."

To his credit, Nathaniel maintained a straight face. "They don't breathe oxygen. They don't have noses or mouths."

Kingsley whacked him over the head with the hilt of her sword. "They're made of fire and oxygen is what keeps fire burning, you nitwit. Don't they teach anything in school anymore?"

The vampire rubbed his head. "I went to school in the 1800s."

"That's no excuse," she shot back. "Any other suggestions for those of us unable to deprive them of oxygen?"

"Brute force?" one of the hulking vampires asked hopefully.

"Water," Nathaniel said. "Though that takes longer. They're more resistant to it."

"There's no water in a place like this," Oren said. "I suppose that's why they've been able to thrive here."

"Callie is the only one who can conjure water here," Nathaniel said.

"Yeah, but I don't conjure water out of thin air." Okay, well I kind of did, except I needed to extract it from moisture in the environment and this place wasn't exactly tropical. "I can manipulate air, though, so I should be able to deplete their oxygen levels low enough to extinguish them."

Kingsley cast an approving look at me. "Well, aren't you full of awesome surprises?"

The flame giants continued to stomp toward us and I focused on the one in the middle. I held up my hands, palms out, and pulled at the concentration of air inside the giant. I'd had plenty of experience with using air-related magic against demons recently. It seemed to be a theme.

My attempt was met with resistance, so I pulled harder. Sweat bubbled on my brow and I wasn't sure whether it was from the approaching heat or the effort involved.

Kingsley hefted her sword. "Are you going to be able to handle this, pumpkin, or do we need to get my plastic surgeon on speed dial?"

I kept my attention on the flame giant and drew the air toward me. The middle giant stumbled and collapsed, although it continued to burn.

Two vampires cheered and high-fived over my head.

I shifted to the giant on the left.

"A little faster, perhaps?" Oren said. "I'm beginning to feel rather hot."

"Maybe back up and put more distance between you and them," I ground out. It was hard to talk and maintain complete concentration.

Pulling air molecules from the fire was like plucking hair from a scalp one at a time. It wasn't as easy as accessing water.

The second flame giant slowed considerably as I strained to extract the last of the oxygen from its form. The third giant continued to advance, seemingly oblivious to the fate of its companions.

"They're like fiery robots," Kingsley said.

"Lucky for us or they'd be much more difficult to kill," Ingemar said.

Although I was vaguely aware of their voices behind us, I kept my focus on the final giant. The creature was close enough now that my face began to burn. I felt a blister forming on my cheek but ignored the discomfort. My palms trembled as I doubled my efforts to extract more oxygen. The creature was a mere twelve feet away now.

Six feet.

I cried out as I gave a final pull and felt the air whoosh into my palms.

With a satisfying hiss, the flame giant disintegrated.

I sagged with relief.

"If only we'd known what threats awaited us and we could've come better prepared," Ingemar said.

"Yes, we could've had each vampire carry a bucket of water instead of a sword." Kingsley shook her head as if to say 'what an idiot.'

With the flame giants eliminated, we pressed onward.

"This place is pretty big for a pocket dimension," Kingsley complained. "I expected it to be smaller."

"Perhaps the size of a pocket?" Ingemar asked, amused.

"Appearances can be deceiving," Nathaniel said. His nostrils flared as he tried to pick up a scent.

"It's like my bottomless bag," I said. "It has a lot more space than you'd think."

Nathaniel halted in his tracks. "This way." He turned left and I inhaled deeply to identify the smell.

My heart seized as a familiar scent filled my nostrils.

Saxon.

I hurried to fall in step with the werewolf. "Saxon's here."

"I thought we'd already established that," Nathaniel said.

"I know, but to smell him..." I shook my head, unable to

say more. The idea that he was really here and we might save him—save all of them. I felt overwhelmed.

"It's the hybrid, isn't it?" Kingsley asked. "The hot one. Sexon."

"Saxon," I corrected her.

She shrugged indifferently. "Same thing."

"You would think they'd sense our presence," Nathaniel said.

"Maybe they did. We fought those flame giants." On the other hand, there was every chance those flame giants simply lived here and we'd passed through their territory.

"Say, Oren, when you mentioned that dangerous creatures stayed behind," Nathaniel began, "any idea how many?"

I followed his gaze to a group of demons visible in the distance. Despite their dresses and long hair, they moved in sync like soldiers marching onto the battlefield.

"What are they?" Oren asked.

"Yamauba," I said.

"They're attractive for frightening demons," Oren said.

"Do they have a superpower?" Nathaniel asked.

Ingemar observed them calmly from his place beside me. "They don't seem formidable."

I looked at him sideways. "They feast on flesh. I guess you have that in common."

"Oh, come on." Kingsley unsheathed her sword. "Don't they know we're here on a mission?"

Their golden white hair gleamed in the dim light.

"Anything else we should know?" Nathaniel asked.

"They have a second mouth on the tops of their heads," I said. "That's the one they use to chew you up and spit you out."

"Gross," Kingsley said.

The Yamauba came to a halt in a straight line about twenty feet away. Only then did I notice the deep lines in their faces and their rows of sharp teeth. I imagined they had a similar set of jagged teeth in their concealed mouths.

I glanced at Oren. "Not so attractive now, are they?"

The vampire grimaced. It seemed I'd finally found his limit.

Kingsley sauntered forward with an air of confidence that Zeus himself would envy. "Listen up, ladies. Normally I am all about female empowerment and would give you each a high-five for your badassery, but right now you're in our way and I just don't have time to waste."

The demons stared at her with a combination of fascination and fury.

"I'm completely serious right now," Kingsley said. When the demons remained rooted in place, the vampire sighed dramatically. "You can't say I didn't warn you."

Her hand moved so quickly that there was no time to react. The blade sliced across the closest demon's neck with such force that the head flew into the arms of her companion. The second demon looked down at the head in her hands and shrieked. The sound was high-pitched and unyielding.

My hands pressed against my ears. "I think we discovered their superpower," I yelled, just as chaos erupted.

They were ferocious fighters but they had no magic, which meant that I was the main advantage for my team. That fact shouldn't have surprised me. It was the entire reason I was created—to be an elite, multifaceted soldier.

It was hard to observe everything happening around me. I had to stay focused on my own targets. They moved quickly and skillfully. Kingsley's attack had been successful because the demon hadn't expected it. We'd lost that advantage of surprise.

This was the first real opportunity I'd had to use my traits openly outside of practice. No hiding. No softening the blow.

This was an all-out fight and I was free to use any skill in my arsenal.

Although I sensed the movements of my companions, I felt like I was in a realm of my own as I took down the demons one at a time. Fangs on one. Magical fireballs on another.

I hated to admit it but I almost enjoyed myself.

When my last opponent dropped to the ground in a heap, I surveyed the barren landscape to see how my companions had fared. My stomach twisted when I saw a white sleeve covered in dirt and blood.

"Oren!" I rushed over to the boulder where the vampire lay unmoving.

He murmured a response and my spirits lifted. "Thank the gods. I thought you bit the dust."

He dragged himself to a seated position. "No, but it certainly feels that way." He examined his sleeves with disgust. The fabric was torn and bloody. "This is unacceptable. The best dry cleaner in Atlantica City won't be able to mend this."

"Maybe next time don't wear your favorite shirt into battle?"

He adjusted his cufflinks. "I wanted to feel like my best self."

I held out a hand and helped him to his feet.

Kingsley stretched her arms over her head. "That was fine for the pre-show. When's the main event?"

I laughed. "You should've joined the Pride. They could use someone like you on the team."

"No, thanks, sweetie. Those freaks are basically civil servants. I like money."

I gave her a pointed look. "You'd also like a world free of Plague demons, I imagine."

She tightened her ponytail. "Well, duh."

"How big is this place?" one of Ingemar's vampires asked.

Ingemar turned to give him a sharp look. "Is that a complaint I hear, Isaiah?"

The vampire's gaze lowered. "No, sir."

"I don't recall complaining to you when I paid for both of your progeny to attend prestigious four-year universities. Do you?"

Isaiah cleared his throat. "Definitely not, sir. You've always been more than generous."

"Because you're family to me," Ingemar said. "Just as the members of the Pride are family."

"More like distant cousins," Oren murmured.

"Where's Nathaniel?" I asked.

"The werewolf?" Kingsley asked. "He went ahead for recon."

My pulse quickened. "Alone?"

"Nobody else here can shift, can they?" she said.

I decided now wasn't the time to explain my abilities in any detail. We continued onward and I watched for any sign of Nathaniel. I was relieved when I spotted a silhouette in the distance. It was low enough to the ground to be a wolf.

As the figure loped toward us, the silhouette grew taller and four legs became two.

Nathaniel. I flew to him, eager to hear any news.

"They're here," he said, and it took all my self-control not to jump for joy.

"All of them?" I pressed.

"Not sure. They're in a series of caves beyond that hill. You need to do a bit of climbing to get to them…" He eyed my wings. "Well, you don't, but the rest of us do."

"I don't think anyone here has an issue with climbing. Any guards?"

Nathaniel's brow creased. "I didn't see anybody, but there has to be something, doesn't there? Otherwise, why wouldn't they be combing the realm for an escape hatch? It's not like your team is apt to be idle and submissive."

No, definitely not.

"There's no chance it's a trap, is there?" Kingsley appeared behind me and apparently overheard our exchange.

"I don't think they would've needed to abduct the whole of Pandora's Pride to lay a trap," I said. Besides, no one knew about me. For once, I was fairly certain this had nothing to do with my secret.

"Why not kill them?" Nathaniel asked. "Why transport them here of all places?"

"It was probably hard enough to teleport them," I said. "Can you imagine trying to kill all of them? They don't have the same weaknesses. The way you'd kill Purvis isn't the same way you'd kill Doran."

"Then someone wanted them out of the way," Nathaniel mused.

"You say 'someone' like you don't know," Kingsley huffed. "You said that Renee chick teleported them."

I studied the horizon. "Maybe so, but this has Plague demon written all over it. Seems like just desserts, doesn't it? To send the Plague demon hunters to dwell in the realm where the demons were trapped for so long?"

"I love a good revenge story," Kingsley said, warming to the idea.

The rest of the vampires finally caught up to us and we explained the situation.

"So we're going to head to the caves and get them out now," I said, "but be aware that there might be unforeseen obstacles."

Kingsley produced a tube of pink gloss from her pocket and applied it to her full lips.

"What on earth are you doing?" Oren asked in disbelief.

She puckered her lips. "Do you think I'm going to let my ex-girlfriend see me with naked lips?"

"Why not? She's seen you naked everywhere else," I said.

Kingsley pointed the tube at me. "This is why you don't have a significant other." She tucked the tube back into her pocket.

"I do, too," I mumbled. Sort of.

Nathaniel shifted back to wolf form and I took to the air. If there was some kind of invisible barrier, I'd be the first to encounter it. I drew energy from my core to my hands, just to be on the safe side.

I landed on the hard ground in front of the first set of caves. No barrier. No guards. I peered into the cave closest to me. There was nothing inside except a familiar hybrid curled up in a ball in a dark corner.

"Liam?"

The werevamp leaped to his feet as though ready to stave off an attack. "Who? Where?" He lowered his claws when he spotted me. "Well, it's about damn time."

"Is that any way to greet your rescuer?" I reached into my pocket and produced a packet of peanut butter crackers that Nathaniel had distributed earlier.

Liam's eyes dilated at the sight of the crackers. "Have I told you how much I love you?"

I tossed the packet to him. "That's better."

"I've learned a valuable lesson while I've been here," he said, crunching hungrily.

"Dare I ask?"

"Don't envy those princesses waiting around in their towers. It's pure agony and not at all as relaxing as it seems."

A lump formed in my throat. "I've missed you, Liam."

"I can ease your suffering right now," he said. "Just hurry up and get me out of here."

"Callie, is that you?"

Time seemed to stand still at the sound of Saxon's voice. I flew to the neighboring cave, my wings flapping with languid movements.

"Saxon," I heard myself say, but the word sounded garbled to my ears.

I landed at the mouth of his cave and my heart slammed into my chest as I spotted the vampire-angel. Only then did time resume its normal pace. I ached to throw my arms around him and kiss him, but that kind of reunion had to wait.

"How did you find us?" he asked.

"More on that later," I said. "Are you all in these caves?"

"Yes," Liam said, appearing beside me.

"Why are you hanging out here like it's a camping trip if there are no protective wards?" I asked.

Saxon and Liam exchanged glances. "Where do we start?" Saxon said.

"Callie?"

I twisted to see Tate. "Thank the gods."

The witch hugged me. "Are you here as a prisoner, too?"

"No, I've come with reinforcements to rescue you," I said.

"Reinforcements?" Liam asked. "Who's left?"

I offered a vague smile. "You'll see."

"I take it Renee isn't here," I said.

"Ha! It was a dump and run," Liam said. "Nobody in their right mind would want to stay here."

Tate gave him a pointed look. "Nobody in their right mind would want to betray us either, yet here we are."

"What happened to the demons that helped her? Apparently there were smaller demons that helped transport you through the portal." I'd wondered whether we'd encounter any of them upon our arrival, but then got distracted by the flame giants and the Yamauba.

"Never saw any of them," Liam said. "The last thing I

remember was Renee giving me a vitamin potion in her office because she said my potassium level was low."

Tate nodded. "She said the same for me."

"I'm surprised one of you didn't sniff out the sedative." Renee had proven to be a wily one. "So you two weren't in the conference room?"

"No," Tate said. "From what we gather, she got to us first and had us set up at the base of the escalator ready to go. Then she targeted the senior members in the conference room before they caught wind of anything."

"Natasha says she made a mess in the lobby because she still had a little movement left before the paralytic kicked in," Liam added.

"Yeah, I saw that." I should've known Natasha went kicking and screaming even through an attempt at paralysis.

"It was the element of surprise," Tate said. "Without that in her favor, this never would've happened."

"I'm sorry this happened to you," I said, trying not to let my guilt rattle me.

We left their set of caves to find the rest of the team. I was especially relieved to see Nita in one piece.

"What about Jonas?" I asked.

"He's visiting his brother in Seattle, thank the gods," Nita said. "He wouldn't have handled this very well."

I was inclined to agree. The Pride assistant was better suited to lamination than dehydration. I was glad he'd missed the whole ordeal.

Natasha intercepted us along the way. "Didn't think you had it in you, Wendell."

"I wasn't about to leave you here to rot," I said. I didn't want to say more under the circumstances.

Nathaniel had already located Purvis and Abra. Doran emerged from his cave, startled to see two additional supernaturals.

"Calandra," Abra said. Her tone suggested that, naturally, I would show up in a pocket realm and rescue them. Not a hint of surprise.

Doran didn't bother to wipe away the tears in his eyes. "I thought we'd never see you again."

"We can dole out hugs and kisses later, big guy," Liam said, slapping Doran between the wings. "Jailbreak comes first."

"Tasha?" Kingsley screeched. She must've charged down the cliffside after glimpsing Natasha.

The vampire's head swiveled. "*Kingsley's* here?"

"Half the vampires in Atlantica City are here," I said. I pointed to the cliff where most of them were now congregated. "They wanted to help."

Natasha gave them an exaggerated wave. "Well, how about that? I'm not just another pretty face."

"You were always more than that," Kingsley said.

Natasha planted a kiss on the blond vampire's lips that made me regret not greeting Saxon with the same level of enthusiasm.

"There's an empty cave right there," Liam said, jabbing a thumb over his shoulder, "but enter at your own risk."

"Hey, where are Emil and Evadne?" I asked.

Abra and Purvis exchanged the kind of look that made me nauseous.

"They're okay, aren't they?" I couldn't squelch the panic in my voice.

"They're unconscious but alive," Abra said. "Despite our best efforts, we've been unable to undo whatever Renee did to them. I need access to my greenhouse for that."

"I assume she had to keep them from making an exit portal," I said.

"The best we can do is to transport them home and try to heal them there," Doran said.

Nathaniel nodded toward the horde of vampires. "There's plenty of muscle for that."

"No offense to Evadne, but it's probably best she's been in a coma all this time," Liam said. "If I had to listen to her complain, I might've killed her myself."

"We had to listen to you and you're still standing," Tate pointed out.

"Yeah, but I'm charming," Liam shot back. "Evadne's just annoying."

"Once we're back at headquarters, I'm sure I can rouse them," Abra said. "As you can imagine, I have nothing here to work with."

"All part of the plan, I bet," Tate said.

"Why not use the same hole the Plague demons used to escape the first time?" Nathaniel asked.

"Doran and I flew all over searching for it," Saxon said. "We kept coming up against other demons and ended up turning back."

"We thought we would locate the hole first and identify potential threats, then we could make a plan," Abra said. "But it wouldn't be easy with two bodies to carry and protect. Tate and I were the only ones with magic."

"That's not strictly true," Doran muttered.

"What about Lloyd?" I asked.

"He isn't here," Abra said. "He left for London the night before the attack."

"You don't think…" I hated to say the words out loud.

Abra understood. "Absolutely not. It was my idea to send him to London as my representative at a witches and wizards council meeting. I never attend in person because that would require leaving Pride headquarters."

At least Lloyd was safe. I was fond of the older wizard.

Liam scratched the back of his neck, chuckling. "Can you

imagine the look on the old geezer's face if he showed up at headquarters?"

"Let's laugh about it in the safety of our rooms," Tate said. She shot me an apprehensive look. "I assume you have a way out for us?"

There was an awkward pause before I found my voice. "I do. There will be a portal waiting at the top of the cliff where the vampires are." If I could create the portal without their eyes on me, it would be best for now. There'd be too many questions from my friends and now wasn't ideal for that particular conversation.

"You brought a fae with you? Is it Harmony?" Liam asked hopefully.

"Harmony can't make portals, so no."

"Someone help me with Emil and Evadne," Saxon said, and I was grateful for the well-timed interruption.

Natasha examined her lengthy nails. "I know exactly what I intend to do when we get back."

"A manicure?" Liam quipped.

Natasha snarled. "Not before I use these nails to dig the heart right out of Renee's chest."

"Do you really think Renee is the mastermind behind this?" Purvis asked with a shake of his shaggy head. "Not a chance."

"My money's on a Plague demon," Liam said.

I balked. "You think you were beaten by one Plague demon and his fae accomplice?"

Abra offered a small smile. "Beaten? I beg to differ. You're here, aren't you?"

I knew what that smile meant. It was the closest the witch would get too smug. As far as she was concerned, this whole rescue mission proved that I was exactly who they intended me to be.

"I couldn't have done this without help." I angled my head

toward the vampires and Nathaniel.

Doran shook Ingemar's hand. "We are in your debt."

"Not at all," Ingemar said. "You would have done the same for any of us."

"We need you in Atlantica City," Kingsley said. "We need you in the human realm."

"I need me in the human realm," Liam said. "That's where all the food is."

I managed to return to the clifftop ahead of them and create the portal. They were so focused on heading home that no one queried the portal's origin. Abra wisely avoided eye contact as she stepped through the glowing circle.

We arrived back at headquarters exhausted but alive and all in one piece. Emil and Evadne were delivered to the recovery rooms adjacent to the healer's office and the rest of the team dragged themselves to their respective rooms.

Saxon squeezed my arm on his way to the elevator bank. "We'll talk later?"

I felt a tightness form across my chest. I'd been too preoccupied with the rescue mission to think about what came next, but now my emotions rushed to the surface. I forced myself to keep my response light and airy. There was plenty of time for explanations now that he was home and safe.

"Get some rest," I said.

I dumped the surviving weapons in the middle of the lobby. "These belong to you."

I started toward the escalator.

"Calandra. A word, please."

I stopped walking and debated my next move. During my time away, I contemplated what I would say the next time I encountered Abra, but I hadn't come up with anything better than curse words intermingled with 'how could you?'

I turned to face the older witch with my hands planted on

my hips. A defensive posture, I realized, but I was too tired to care.

"I'm pretty beat. Any chance this can wait until tomorrow?"

Her expression was inscrutable. "I only want to thank you. You didn't have to help us. You could've left the vampires to figure it out alone."

"They wouldn't have and you'd all be dead."

"I'm sure you're right."

"I met your sister," I said. "I like her a lot. Not so sure about the tea leaf thing, but…"

Her face registered surprise. "You went to see Marie?"

"I would've stayed longer, but the Order of Beltane crashed the party."

She frowned. "And the coven?"

"They're fine. Everyone's fine." I paused. "She reminded me of you. I think she misses you. I told her about Tate."

The witch clenched and unclenched her hands. "I suppose you talked about the reason I left."

"The reason you were expelled? Yeah, she might've mentioned it."

Abra clasped her hands in front of her. "Perhaps we can meet again tomorrow when we're both feeling more civilized?"

"So you can torture me until I agree to return? I don't think so."

"There is more at stake than your identity crisis," Abra said. "Given all that's happened, I would've thought…"

"Well, you thought wrong," I interrupted. Anger flooded me and I felt the muscles in my neck tighten. "If you think I'm only angry because of the lies you handed out like cocaine at a nightclub, then you don't know me very well."

Abra took a hesitant step closer. "Enlighten me."

"What you did…The steps you were willing to take…" I

shook my head, struggling to find the words. "You're no better than the Order of Beltane. You're an extremist, determined to achieve your goal at any price. Well, I am here to tell you that the cost is too high. You have to find another way."

We stared at each other for what seemed like an eternity. Part of me wondered whether she'd attack. I was more powerful but worn out from fighting and portal-making. Abra had more experience. Tension crawled through every muscle in my body, but I refused to break eye contact or show any sign of weakness.

"What do you suggest?" she finally asked.

I blinked in confusion. "What do you mean?"

She unclasped her hands. "You're telling me to find another way, to leave the Sunstone be. I'm asking you what you propose as an alternative."

"For starters, we have an immediate threat. You don't have twenty years to modify and brainwash a bunch of innocent children."

"An accurate assessment."

I glanced at the weapons on the floor. "We take them out. All of them."

She burst into laughter. "What do you think we've been doing all these years?"

"No, not with weapons. Not as the need arises." I met her gaze. "We find a way to send them back where they came from in—one fell swoop."

Abra's brow wrinkled. "The magic required..."

I waved her off. "We don't have to come up with a solution right now." I could barely come up with the strength to breathe at this point, let alone a plan to save the world.

"A truce then?" she asked.

I hesitated and she saw the look of apprehension on my face.

"You don't trust me," she said flatly.

"Can you blame me?"

"I suppose not."

"Have you told them?" I asked, gesturing to the elevators which the rest of the team had taken to their rooms.

"Not yet."

"After you wake up Emil and Evadne, you tell them," I said firmly. "Because if you don't, I will."

CHAPTER TEN

I STUDIED the cracks in the ceiling of my hotel room and tried to decompress. Oren had been kind enough to send room service, but I'd left it in the hallway untouched. I was too stressed to eat. Although the rescue mission had been successful, it wouldn't be without consequences. My friends would be devastated when they learned the truth about themselves—about Pandora's Pride. They had to be told, though. My father always said the right thing to do was usually the same as the hard thing and recent events proved him to be a wise man yet again.

Duncan Waite. Quinn Wendell.

Both my father.

A soft tapping at my window interrupted my thoughts and I knew without looking that Saxon was outside.

One glimpse of his face and it was clear he knew.

I opened the window and let him inside.

"Callie." His expression was so pained that I started to cry.

He collapsed against me and I held onto him for dear life. "I'm so sorry. I wanted to tell you, but it didn't seem right coming from me."

He pressed his head against my chest, seemingly desperate for comfort. "I didn't understand why you left…"

I lifted his chin to look at him. "And now you do?"

"I want you to know that I wasn't a part of it. They kept us in the dark, too."

"I know that." I curled my fingers in his hair. "The elders kept it to themselves because they knew what everyone would think."

He shifted to his full height forcing my gaze upward. I reached up to stroke his chiseled jaw.

"I wasn't born this way," he choked out. "They made me into something else."

I fought against the swell of emotions that threatened to drown me. I'd had my time to fall apart. Right now, I needed to support Saxon and be a source of strength for him. He would've done the same for me if I'd let him.

"You're perfect," I said. I reached behind his shoulder to stroke the feathers of his wing. "Every last bit of you is perfect."

I climbed on the bed and made room for him beside me. Wordlessly, he joined me and rested his cheek on my chest.

"They're not who I thought they were," he whispered. "Hell, I'm not even who I thought I was."

I kissed him lightly on the lips. "You are, Saxon."

"Do you mind if I stay here tonight?"

I gazed into his mismatched eyes. "Stay as long as you like. What about the others?"

He squeezed his eyes closed. "I don't know. I stormed out first. I should've checked on them."

I cupped his cheek in my hand. "No. You're the team captain in the field, but not for this. You need to come to terms, too."

"Is it true that you have every trait?" he asked, peering at me with curiosity.

"Apparently. I've been working my way through them."

He seemed momentarily awestruck. "It explains so much."

"It does." I told him about my father and Nathaniel. About my conversation with Abra in the greenhouse and the importance of the Sunstone. Any detail that the inner circle omitted, I filled in.

Saxon gazed at me in wonder. "I can't imagine how you must've felt."

"Pretty similar to the way you feel right now, I suspect," I said. "I went to Massachusetts to visit Abra's former coven."

His brow lifted. "That's where you disappeared to?"

"Until the Order of Beltane spoiled the party. I couldn't stay there and bring danger to their doorstep again."

"The Order is right," he said quietly. "We are abominations."

"We're not," I insisted. "We're good and compassionate and hard-working. We're what others aspire to be and what demons can never be."

"I can't believe you risked your life to rescue them after everything they did to you," he said.

"I wasn't about to leave you there," I said. "My feelings for them may be complicated, but not my feelings for you." Or for my friends. They were innocent in all this, too.

The next kiss left me in no doubt as to whether Saxon returned my feelings. Strong fingers gripped my shoulder as the pressure of our lips intensified. We seemed to be pouring all our emotions into a single kiss. When we finally broke apart, a chill came over me and I snuggled closer to him for warmth.

"I should check on the others," he said.

I didn't try to dissuade him this time. He wasn't just their team captain; he cared about them. We both did.

Before he could retrieve his phone from his pocket, there was a knock on the door. I shot him a quizzical look before sliding off the bed and padding across the floor to answer it.

I peered through the peephole to see Tate and Liam huddled together outside the door. Exhaling with relief, I opened the door and let them in.

Tate hooked her arms around my neck and hugged me fiercely.

"Should've known we'd find you here," Liam said, noticing Saxon in the room. He'd moved off the bed to stand in front of the window.

"How are you?" I asked them. Tate's face was blotchy and Liam seemed to be holding tension in his shoulders and fists. Other than that, they looked like their usual selves.

"How am I? A dangerous question, my friend." Tate perched on the edge of the bed. "I'm so angry right now, I want to rip a hole in the fabric of reality and shove my grandmother straight through it."

Liam whistled. "Tell us how you really feel, Tate. No need to hold back."

"The way Natasha tried to justify everything..." Tate grimaced. "She should have been pleading with us for forgiveness."

"She didn't apologize?" I queried. I had wondered what approach they might take when the time came.

"Ha!" Liam said. "Natasha doesn't know the meaning of the word."

"How can they apologize?" Tate asked. "They'd lose their air of authority and superiority."

"At least you're still you," Liam said to the witch.

"They still lied to me, Liam," Tate shot back. "My own grandmother still admitted to doing terrible things for the sake of the world."

"You had no idea?" I asked.

Tate scrunched her nose and mouth. "I trusted them. It never occurred to me to question things."

I couldn't fault her for that. I'd been exactly the same with my father and Nathaniel. Even if a question had nagged at me on occasion, I'd likely found a way to dismiss it in my own head before it ever escaped my lips. I had no reason to question what I'd been told.

"Where's Evadne?" I asked.

No one answered.

"Let me try this again. Where is Evadne?" I asked.

"She left," Tate said.

"What happened? She flipped out when they told her that her fae side came from Emil and not some mysterious ancestor?"

"Something like that," Liam said. "She may have flipped a few pieces of furniture, too. And the bird. Lots of flipping."

"I was surprised she didn't attack Natasha," Tate said. "Those two looked ready to come to blows."

"They're going to have more than Plague demons to contend with if they can't convince Evadne to see reason," Saxon said.

"Do *you* see reason?" Tate asked.

"The only thing I see right now is red," Saxon admitted. "It's why I came here to cool off. And it seems I wasn't the only one with that idea."

"Where would Evadne go to cool off?" I asked. Although I knew the tri-brid could handle herself, I worried about her state of mind. If Nathaniel hadn't been there to offer emotional support after I learned the truth, I had no idea what I might've done.

"Knowing her, she's pummeling the crap out of some thug vampire she encountered in a dark alley," Liam said. "We should leave her to it."

I pressed my lips together, thinking. If anything bad

happened to Evadne because everyone left her to her own devices, we'd never forgive ourselves.

"I think we should look for her," I said.

Liam shook his head. "I'm not volunteering for that thankless job. She'd probably kick my ass just for caring about her."

"I'll go on my own then," I said. "You're welcome to stay here. In fact..." I dug out my phone and called Oren. "Hey, it's Callie. Would it be possible to book the adjacent room to this one?"

"You're not going to make me share a room with Liam, are you?" Tate looked aghast. "I've been traumatized enough today."

"Thanks, buddy. You're the best." I put away the phone and addressed the room. "Saxon and Liam can have the room next door. Oren said it has two queen beds."

Saxon appeared disappointed at the prospect of being separated from me, but there wasn't much I could about it at the moment.

"I'll let you know when I find Evadne," I said.

I dipped into the bathroom to brush my hair and make myself presentable.

"Can we order room service?" Liam called as I reached the door.

"Knock yourself out."

When I reached the lobby, I stopped by the security desk and asked them to call me if they spotted someone matching Evadne's description. I wouldn't put it past her to start a brawl in the middle of the pit.

I spilled onto the boardwalk and walked the length of it in search of the tri-brid. I had a feeling Evadne would make her presence known tonight wherever she went. She wasn't exactly the type to swallow her feelings.

On second thought...

I left the boardwalk at the nearest ramp and headed into the heart of the city. There was one place Evadne *would* swallow her feelings, followed by a tequila chaser or two.

I spread my wings and flew several blocks to my destination. It still felt strange to be able to fly with such ease. To produce wings and fangs and whatever else I wanted just by willing it into existence. The Pride had tested me repeatedly without me realizing it. Once the inhibitor potion had completely left my system, they had been eager to see what I could do. Of course, they'd had to do it discreetly. They hadn't wanted to risk me noticing but the only way they could achieve that was by putting me under intense emotional pressure. Once I'd accessed those hidden parts of myself, it got easier every time. I'd spent night after night tucked in my bedroll, willing my fangs to appear and levitating off the ground. I'd drawn the line at eavesdropping on Nathaniel's thoughts. Telepathy didn't appeal to me, although it might've saved me a lot of heartache if I'd been able to read thoughts before I arrived in Atlantica City.

I landed outside Twinkle Twinkle Little Bar as patrons fled the local watering hole.

"I think I found her," I said, maneuvering through the throng of bodies.

A man grabbed my arm in an effort to stop me. "You don't want to go in there. She's nuts. She'll kill you."

I shook myself free and continued into the now-empty bar where a bartender cowered behind the counter. Tables had been overturned and chairs knocked on their sides. I turned toward the stage and sighed. The only thing Evadne was in danger of killing was the song she was about to sing.

The music started and Evadne clutched the microphone in both hands. "Desperado," she warbled.

Oh boy.

I strolled over to the bar and sat atop a stool. "A tankard of your finest ale, please."

The bartender slowly rose to her feet. "Are you sure?" Her gaze darted to the stage where Evadne continued to sing, oblivious to my entrance.

"If you want, you can go and I'll get it myself."

She seemed at a loss. "I don't know…"

"She won't hurt you," I said. "She just needs to let off some steam."

"She was pretty angry," the bartender said, pulling me a pint. "She stormed in here yelling like a madwoman. It was only when she started knocking over tables that everyone took notice of her."

"And wisely fled."

"She made me turn on the karaoke machine," the bartender said.

"I used to hear this song a lot in dive bars in the mountains." I listened to Evadne's version and resisted the urge to cringe. "It sounded a little different from this though."

The bartender smiled and seemed to relax.

I swallowed a mouthful of ale and watched Evadne hum her way through the rest of the song. It wasn't as though the lyrics were too complicated to remember.

Her gaze finally landed on me. "Callie," she said directly into the microphone and my name reverberated throughout the bar.

I patted the empty stool beside me.

"You sure about this?" the bartender asked.

"Leave a pitcher and an empty glass here and feel free to hide in the back," I told her.

The bartender wasted no time doing just that as Evadne hopped off the stage and hauled herself over to me. She set the microphone on the counter with a loud thud that echoed.

"Might want to turn that off," I said.

She flicked the button on the side without a glance. "That for me?" She angled her head toward the glass.

I tipped the pitcher forward and poured the ale, hoping not to spill any. The slightest thing could set her off if I wasn't careful. Although I felt confident I could keep her in check, there was always a chance I was wrong.

"No one else wanted to find me, huh?" She gulped down half the glass and then dragged her sleeve across her mouth.

"They're letting you cool off."

She leaned an elbow on the counter. "I nailed that song."

"You were incredible. I felt every note."

"You're a weird one, Callie Wendell."

I took a sip of ale. "Oh? How's that?"

"You find out you've been kidnapped, deceived, experimented on—all sorts of complete and utter bullshit—and you still found your way to hell and back so you could rescue us."

I lifted my glass. "The key word in that sentence is *us*."

She drank more. "You can't fool me. You would've gone anyway, even if it was Abra all by her lonesome."

I wasn't so sure, but it wasn't worth arguing about. "I'm here to talk about you, Evadne."

She grunted. "And what? Make sure I don't murder a bar full of innocents in a drunken haze of anger? Not to worry." The tri-brid patted my arm and nearly missed connecting with it. "I'm too pissed off to hurt anyone." She sat upright and made a face. "Wait. That doesn't make any sense."

"I know how upsetting this must be for you."

"I bet you do." Evadne polished off the rest of her ale and refilled the glass. "I knew you had a good reason for leaving, but I didn't guess what it was. I assumed Saxon broke up with you like the dutiful team captain he is."

There was no point in denying a relationship now. Abra and her cohorts had lost the right to make those kinds of rules.

"He didn't break up with me. I left without telling him the reason."

She aimed her glass at me. "The Sunstone is part of their scheme, isn't it? They didn't tell us that pacifically…" She paused. "Specifically. But I put two and two together."

"It was used for their most successful project."

"You?"

"Your daddy stole it when he ran off with you and then hid you both."

"That about sums it up."

Evadne laughed as she swiveled to face the counter. "I like your dad. I wish I could've met him so I could shake his hand."

"He would've liked you, too."

She barked a laugh. "No one likes me. Hell, I don't even like myself most of the time. Now I know why." She slumped over her glass. "I don't know what to do, Callie."

"You don't have to make any decisions now," I assured her. "Just give yourself time to process."

"I don't know. The more time I have to think, the angrier I get. I don't care that I'm a freak of nature." She tipped back the glass and sucked down more of the golden liquid. "If they'd given me the option to volunteer for this, I would have."

"But you don't like the lies."

She turned her head toward me. "I can put up with a lot of nonsense, but lies from the ones who are supposed to take care of you. The ones who send you into danger on a regular basis." She heaved a sigh. "We're sacrificial lambs, Callie. That's all we ever were to them. Even Leto."

I finished my drink and shifted the glass aside to avoid knocking it over.

"I think that's why Tate and Leto aren't hybrids," Evadne

continued. "They had the decency to draw the line at experimenting on their own kin."

"But not the decency to keep them out of harm's way," I said pointedly. Otherwise Leto would still be alive.

"Why are you still here?" Evadne asked. "You and Saxon should be halfway to Vegas by now."

I stifled a laugh. "Why Vegas?"

"I don't know. Seems like the kind of place you escape to, doesn't it?"

"Do you think you might go there?" I wanted to get a sense of where Evadne's head was at the moment. If she disappeared tomorrow, I'd already have a lead.

"Here's the thing, Wendell. I like what I do. I'm good at it and I can't imagine doing anything else."

"You're fortunate to have that."

"Yeah, but how can I possibly go back to headquarters and work for them, knowing the truth? I'm nothing but a weapon to them. An object to use for their own purposes. They covet the Sunstone more than they covet me, especially now when they can make more of you."

"It's not an ideal situation."

"Understatement of the year, Callie Wendell," she yelled, waving her glass back and forth with a flourish. She took another swig and set down the glass. "Are you as powerful as they say?"

"That depends."

Evadne frowned. "On what?"

"On whether you're going to want me to prove it."

She knocked my shoulder. "You I believe. You didn't come here with a hidden agenda. You were all about avenging your dad and got tangled up with this group." She shook her head sadly. "Maybe you should've left us in the other realm."

"Plague demons are still out there," I said. "That wouldn't have been the right call."

She eyed me. "For the greater good? You've been spending too much time with Abra if you're willing to trade everything for the greater good. At least hang on to your self-respect. You want it to be worth something." She hiccupped and laughed. "I think I'll sing another one. How do you feel about power ballads?"

"I think we should leave and let the poor bartender go home. She's had a rough night."

Evadne's gaze shifted to the stage. "Do what you want. I'm singing a Celine Dion song before I head out. These supernatural lungs were made for belting out a tune."

I knocked once on the counter. "I'll leave you to it then. Don't strain your vocal cords." I left a wad of bills on the counter and sauntered to the door as Evadne returned to the stage with the microphone in hand.

CHAPTER ELEVEN

THE NEXT MORNING, I wasn't surprised to learn that Evadne skipped town.

"Nita texted me," Tate said. She hugged the pillow as she sat cross-legged on the bed. "Evadne left on a bus early this morning."

The tri-brid likely never went to bed last night.

"Nita spoke to her?" I asked.

"Not sure. Apparently Evadne tried to steal one of the Pride vehicles first and ended up at the bus station."

"Which vehicle?" Liam asked.

Tate huffed. "Does it really matter? She didn't take it."

"Good because I'd have to hunt her down myself," Liam said.

"Why wouldn't she portal?" Saxon asked.

"Probably the bus has a better chance at taking her to her destination," Liam shot back.

Tate tucked her chin toward her chest. "We'll lose her forever," she said.

"We won't," I said. "I have a feeling I know where she's headed."

Tate tossed the pillow aside and leaped out of bed, her eyes bright. "Then we should go after her."

I patted her shoulder. "Calm down, mother hen. We're going to let her go for now."

Slowly, she sank back to the mattress. "We are?"

I nodded. "We are. She'll be fine. She just needs time to process and she's going to do that differently from you or Saxon or Liam."

"Or you," Tate added.

"Or me," I agreed.

"If we end up with a trail of bodies…" Saxon began.

"We won't." I knew Evadne would behave herself, at least to the extent that she wouldn't go on a murder spree. On the other hand, I expected quite a few eardrums in karaoke bars to suffer.

Liam stared at the coffee machine. "You mean I have to make it myself?"

"That's generally how it works," I said.

He looked back at me. "Can one of you magic it?"

Tate snorted. "Talk about privileged."

"Allow me." I brushed past him and started the machine the old-fashioned way. "How are you all feeling? I feel like we should talk it out."

"What is there to say?" Saxon leaned his back against the window, his arms folded across his chest. "They took advantage of innocent children. Lied to us."

"I could've been an accountant," Liam said.

"No, you couldn't have," Tate shot back. "That requires math skills that you don't possess."

He shook a sugar packet in anticipation. "But I might've possessed them if I hadn't been trained to kill instead."

I slid the cup over to him and he inhaled the aroma before dumping in two packets of sugar.

"You just annihilated that coffee," Saxon said.

"Better the coffee than our esteemed members of the Pride," Liam replied.

Three phones buzzed at the same time while mine remained silent. No psychic skills necessary to know who was calling.

The other three exchanged glances.

"Someone's ballsy," Liam said.

Tate shook her head adamantly. "I can't deal with them right now."

Saxon stared at the phone in his hand. "I don't want to either, but there's a demon out there intent on waging war on us and we're the best chance at stopping him. Whatever's about to happen is bigger than what happened to us."

Tate's face softened. "Your identity...Your life is important, too."

"I know that, but it doesn't help anybody to stew in resentment about what could've been while the world burns."

Liam rolled his eyes. "You can take the hero out of headquarters..." He scratched his head. "Wait, that doesn't work."

The phones ceased buzzing.

"You're going to go, aren't you?" Tate asked.

Saxon peeled his back off the window. "It doesn't mean I condone what they did or that I've forgiven them, but there are plenty of innocent children out there now who don't deserve what might happen to them if we don't intervene. The greater good has to come first."

"That's the Pride mantra," Liam said. "I guess they brainwashed us pretty good."

"It's not a bad thing, to choose a life that serves others," I said. "It would've just been better if we got to choose that role for ourselves."

Tate fiddled with her phone. "What do you think, Callie?"

"I hate to say it, but I think Saxon's right. I think we need to set aside our grievances and save the world."

"Again?" Liam moaned.

I nodded. "Again."

No one was in good spirits when we entered headquarters and no one pretended that we should be. The elders were assembled in the conference room with the usual spread of food on the sideboard. Their faces were appropriately grim.

"Thank you for coming," Doran said. "We know it can't be easy for you to walk back in here."

"We knew this day would come eventually," Emil said.

"I never wanted to keep it a secret in the first place," Natasha snapped, her lip curling slightly. "I was outvoted."

"Gold star for you," Tate said, taking her seat.

Natasha glared at her. "What are you so upset about? You got to stay pure. You and Leto." She shot a pointed look at Abra and I sensed there'd been a disagreement about that as well, many years ago.

Abra remained noticeably silent.

Liam loaded up a plate with every carb available before seating himself at the table.

"As I'm sure you're aware, Evadne has taken leave of us," Emil said.

I didn't offer the reassurances that I'd given to the others. They didn't deserve it.

"Why are we here?" Saxon asked. "Is there news on the demon responsible?"

"Not yet, but we want to keep you informed as to next steps."

"So now you want to be open and honest with us?" Liam asked, stuffing a bagel into his mouth. "Okay then."

"I intend to do a locator spell this morning." Abra rolled her fingers along the strand of pearls around her neck. "If

Renee is back in this realm, it should be easy enough for me to find her."

"And you can give that address straight to me," Natasha said.

Abra nodded. "Consider it done."

I shifted uncomfortably in my seat. The menacing gleam in Natasha's eye left me in no doubt as to the vampire's intentions. Renee was going to pay for her role in the Pride's abduction.

"I don't mind helping you with that locator spell," I piped up. I figured Abra would be reluctant to turn down my offer of assistance given everything that happened between us.

"An excellent idea," Abra said. Her tight smile suggested otherwise, but I didn't care. I got what I wanted.

"We also want to offer a formal apology." Doran glanced at his colleagues. "We know that we took liberties that perhaps we shouldn't have, but we were desperate for a solution."

"And we were expendable," Liam said. "Yeah, we got it."

"On the contrary, Liam," Abra said. "We view you as essential members of our mission."

"And that's how you viewed us as children, too," Liam said. "And therein lies the problem."

"You're welcome to say whatever you need to say to us," Purvis interrupted. "To handle this however you deem fit going forward. We only ask that you work with us to eliminate the immediate threat. Someone capable of spiriting the entire team away from headquarters is capable of much, much worse."

"We agree and that's the reason we came," Saxon said.

Abra offered a crisp nod. "Excellent. I'll be in touch as soon as I have the fae's location."

I pushed back my chair. "*We'll* be in touch."

The younger team members vacated the room first and I quickly pulled them into a huddle by the elevator bank.

"We need to get to Renee first," I said.

"Why?" Tate asked. "Natasha said she was going to take care of it."

"Seriously, let her handle a task for a change," Liam said.

"Natasha isn't going to *handle a task*," I said. "Natasha is going for the jugular."

"Good point," Liam said. "I want in on that action."

I slammed a hand against his chest. "No, that's not what I mean. We have to get to her first so we can get information. If Natasha waltzes in and kills her before we get answers, bye-bye last link to the demon responsible."

Saxon rubbed his jaw. "I agree with Callie."

"Shocker," Liam said.

"I'm going to meet Abra in the greenhouse, but I want you all to be ready on my signal because we're going to have to hurry to beat Natasha."

"Got it," Liam said. "In the meantime, I'll be outside. Being in here is making my skin crawl."

Saxon lightly touched my arm. "Are you sure you'll be okay alone with Abra?"

I forced a smile. "The greater good, right?"

He gave me a lingering look before following the others out of the building.

Abra was only a minute behind me arriving at the greenhouse.

"Never thought I'd be back in this room," I said in an effort to ease the tension.

"I have to admit I thought the same thing." Abra crossed the aisle to a row of leafy plants and herbs. I watched as she swept a basket off the floor and added bits of rosemary and basil. Then she tossed in a few sandalwood chips. "It isn't a difficult spell for someone of your caliber, but performance is the key to perfecting it."

I recognized Renee's toothbrush on the table and realized that Abra had swiped it from the healer's bathroom.

"I used hair from her brush to form a link with the pocket realm," I said.

"That was very clever," Abra said. "I was interested to hear all about your methods, but didn't feel I could pry." Her hands moved quickly and efficiently, adding bristles from the toothbrush into a copper pot filled with leaves. She added a drop from a pre-mixed potion bottle labeled 'locator' and stirred the concoction with a cinnamon stick.

"Maybe we should get this on the menu at the coffee shop," I joked.

My eyes bulged as Abra lifted the small pot to her lips and drank. I was only kidding. I didn't expect her to actually imbibe.

Abra's eyes fluttered closed and she swayed to the left before straightening. I scooped the pot from her hands before she dropped it.

A moment later her eyes opened.

"She isn't far," Abra said. "Surprising. I expected her to be on the other side of the world by now."

"Would it matter? We could portal anywhere to get to her and she knows it." And so could Renee.

"She's in an apartment in Wilmington, Delaware." Abra reeled off the address. "I'll have Emil prepare the portal."

"Do you think it's wise to leave this to Natasha?" I asked. "Isn't it more important to get answers?"

"Oh, we fully intend to get answers, Calandra."

I understood. They'd extract the answers and then turn a blind eye to whatever Natasha did next.

"She violated our trust," Abra said, as though that excused Natasha's plan for revenge.

"Yeah, maybe you should ruminate on that," I said pointedly. I left the greenhouse in a hurry and alerted the team to the location. I instructed them to meet me a block from headquarters so that no one saw our portal.

Unfortunately, we didn't beat Natasha to the location.

The door to the apartment hung off its hinges and we crammed inside the small studio. Renee was in the middle of the floor encased in a magical box of light to keep herself safe from Natasha. Props for quick thinking.

A bruise had already started to form on Renee's forehead. Natasha must've taken her by surprise with a fist to the head.

The vampire's eyes gleamed with anger. "Good, you're here. Get rid of that magic shield so I can throttle her."

"Did she tell you who's behind your abduction?" I asked.

"*She* infiltrated our safe space and *she* created the portal that took us away," Natasha ground out.

"I had no choice," Renee cried out from her place on the floor.

Natasha jerked back to the fae. "There's always a choice and you, my dear fool, chose poorly."

Saxon positioned himself between Natasha and Renee. "If you kill her, many innocent people will die."

"Isn't that the whole point of the Pride?" I added. "To save the innocent from hell on earth?"

Natasha hesitated, her gaze darting from us to the fae. Finally, she took a step backward and motioned to Renee. "Your witness, counselor."

Saxon crouched so that he was eye level with Renee. "We don't want to hurt you."

Renee barked a laugh. "I beg to differ."

"Look, we just need to know who you're working for," Saxon said. "If you tell us, we'll leave."

"I can't tell you," Renee said. Tears streamed down her cheeks.

"Are you under a spell?" Tate asked. "If so, we can find a way to break it."

Renee shook her head and wiped the wetness from her face.

"If your boss doesn't kill you, I will, so you might as well help the good guys." Natasha's fangs glinted in the dim light.

An idea occurred to me. "She isn't worried about her own death." I joined Saxon on the floor in front of the shield. "You're worried about your daughter, aren't you?"

"Daughter?" Liam asked.

The emotional dam burst and Renee's choking sobs broke through. "Courtney. Varcin has her and refused to release her unless I helped him with his plan. She's been gone for months."

"Why didn't you tell us that when you came to us?" Saxon asked. "We could've helped you."

Renee tried to regain her composure. "He said he was watching my every move and that Courtney would be dead within minutes of my betrayal."

"Varcin," Natasha repeated. "That's his name?"

She sniffed and nodded. "Plague demon. He chose everything. Timing. Location. Plan."

"What's his bigger plan?" I asked. "Why transport the Pride to the pocket realm?"

"I don't know the larger plan," Renee said. "I came to Wilmington after I fulfilled my end of the bargain."

"Why hasn't he released her?" Natasha asked. "Could it be because you're lying through those ridiculously straight white teeth?"

Renee's eyes welled with tears. "Because he knows you escaped. He blames me for that. He said I shouldn't have left loose threads." Her gaze drifted to me before returning to Natasha.

"So what now?" Natasha asked. "You hang out here waiting for your next orders?"

Renee's head bobbed. "He said he'd give me one more chance to make it right before he killed her."

"And what are the orders?" Saxon asked.

"He hasn't issued them yet," Renee said. "I have to wait here. I'm not allowed to leave for any reason. All my food comes via a delivery service."

"This is good," I said.

Natasha glowered. "You and I have different definitions of good."

"We let Renee await her instructions and that brings us one step closer to Varcin and his next step," I said.

Natasha's jaw tightened. "As much as I would love to sink my fangs into your sweet fae flesh, Callie's right. Varcin is the bigger target."

Renee trembled. "I'll do whatever you need, I swear."

"You'd better or you'll live to regret it." Natasha ran her tongue over her upper lip. "Or on second thought, you won't."

"I can't call you," Renee said. "He'll know."

"Doran or I will make contact," I said. Varcin wouldn't be able to track her dreams.

"Please help," Renee said. "Courtney is innocent. If I'd stopped gambling…"

"What happened? You lost her in a poker game?" Saxon asked, aghast.

Renee averted her gaze. "Not exactly. Varcin offered to wipe my debts clean if I did this one job for him. That's how he found me. When I refused, he took Courtney."

I felt awful for Renee. As much as I condemned her actions, I recognized she was in a tough situation. She didn't deserve to die for trying to save her daughter.

We left the apartment with a plan in place and I was relieved that Natasha came without resistance.

"How do we make sure she doesn't rat us out to Varcin?" Saxon asked, once we were outside the building.

"She won't," Natasha said. "She'll be too frightened of repercussions from both sides. Varcin might blame her for letting herself be found."

"Abra thought it was strange that she didn't flee the area," I said. "Now we know why."

Natasha squeezed my shoulder. "You got my brains, that's for sure." When I glared at her, she arched an eyebrow. "Too soon?"

"At least we have a name," Tate said. "That's huge."

Liam rolled up imaginary sleeves. "Let's go find him."

The vampire's expression turned sour. "Varcin and his buddies are going to pay for what they did. Every last one of them."

"Varcin wanted us out of the way so he can—what? March a demon army across every country?" Tate asked.

"Our own demonic Napoleon," Liam said, his shoulders sagging. "Terrific."

CHAPTER TWELVE

WE RETURNED to Atlantica City as a group. Natasha didn't bother to ask if we'd accompany her to headquarters. She knew better, so the vampire went solo to update the Pride on Renee's revelation and assign Nita a new research project while the rest of us remained huddled on the boardwalk.

"I've never heard of Varcin," Tate said. She hopped up and down in an effort to stay warm.

"Nuts?" Liam asked, angling his head toward the vendor selling roasted chestnuts.

"We certainly are," Tate said. "And yes. I'm hungry."

Liam trotted over to purchase a bag. Now that the weather had turned colder, the roasted chestnuts were even more satisfying.

"Whoever he is, he's a pretty formidable demon," Saxon said.

Tate continued her dance of warmth. "I'll say. He almost beat the Pride and he didn't even show up to gloat."

"Because it wasn't about revenge," I said. "It wasn't even about you, specifically. He's a calculating demon."

Liam rejoined our huddle and thrust a bag at Tate. "Hold these and you'll warm up quickly."

Tate hugged the bag of roasted chestnuts to her body. "Much better. Thanks."

"We can talk inside, you know," I said. "We don't have to torture you out here."

"I didn't feel like being indoors yet," Tate said, crunching on a nut. "The portal made me queasy."

Saxon's phone pinged and he tugged it from his jeans pocket to glance at the screen. "We're back on duty."

Liam tipped his head back and groaned. "Again? I haven't been this exhausted since that pub crawl in London two years ago. Gods above, I was so wasted, I took a bath in the Thames." He chuckled at the memory.

"Yes, because this is the same," Tate said, her tone laced with sarcasm.

Liam reached into the bag for a handful of nuts. "Where to this time, Captain?"

"Nuisance demons in Anaheim," Saxon said. "Emil said to meet him out front and he'll get the portal ready."

"I can make the portal," I said. Inwardly, I cringed. Why did I volunteer? I was supposed to be distancing myself, not offering to help. I was here for the Big Bad and nothing else.

"No thanks," Liam said. "Evadne's bad enough. Your portal will probably take us to the bottom of the ocean."

"I've been practicing," I said. "Nathaniel thinks I've gotten really good."

"He's a werewolf from the hinterlands," Liam scoffed. "What does he know about portals?"

Saxon clapped the werevamp on the shoulder. "Callie is offering to help, Liam. I think maybe we should take her up on it instead of giving her more reasons to regret knowing us."

"I hate to raise a sore subject, but do any of us want to

141

help?" Tate asked. "I mean, we can say no. Be rebellious for once."

"Did they say what kind of demons?" Liam asked.

Tate rolled her eyes. "That's the deciding factor? What about principles?"

Liam stopped crunching. "Principles are the reason I'm asking. Just because I'm twenty-two kinds of pissed doesn't mean I want demons to win."

"Twenty-two?" I queried.

Liam shrugged. "I'm creative."

"They're darvands from the sound of it," Saxon interjected.

"At least we know it's not connected to Varcin," Liam said.

I looked at him. "How can you be sure?"

"Because darvands wouldn't be able to take over a convenience store unless the clerk handed them the keys. They're nuisance demons."

"There sure has been an influx of nuisance demon reports in the last month," Tate said. "Don't they know we have Plague demons to worry about?"

I frowned. "Does anyone think it's odd that Varcin hasn't made another move yet?"

"He's probably regrouping after his failed attempt on us," Tate said.

I scooped nuts from the bag. "Does that make sense to you? That Varcin would plan far enough ahead to get a fae installed at Pride headquarters but not have an immediate Plan B should his capture of you fail?"

"So he's overly confident," Saxon said with a shrug. "Isn't that most demons? Their hubris is what gets them caught half the time."

"And the other half is their stupidity," Liam added.

I shook my head, unconvinced. "We're missing something."

"Right now, we're missing a darvand attack on Anaheim," Saxon said. "If we're committed to helping, then we need to get moving. Doran said he alerted the angels. They have a stronghold nearby and he's hoping they'll send a few reinforcements if the need arises."

I gripped his arm. "Wait. The angels have a stronghold there?"

"About thirty miles away," Saxon said. "Why?"

My mind clicked as pieces began to fall into place. "In North Carolina, the gogome demons that Nathaniel and I encountered..."

Tate's eyes rounded. "They were near a werewolf stronghold."

"Those nuisance demons we fought in Iowa last week were near both a fae compound *and* a werewolf stronghold," Saxon said.

"You missed that one," Liam said to me. "Word to the wise —don't ever get stuck in a corn maze with a gaggle of demons." He shook his head ruefully. "You'll find kernels in places you never dreamed of."

"What if these nuisance demon attacks *are* connected to Varcin?" I asked.

"I don't see how," Liam said.

"I don't know either, but these attacks don't seem random. They could be part of his plan," I said.

Liam cocked his head. "But the attacks have been failing. The demons are small potatoes."

Tate clutched the bag of nuts to her chest. "Unless failure is part of the plan. What if he's testing boundaries? He's choosing places near the most powerful supernatural hubs to see what happens. Who comes to their aid? What security measures are taken? He planned to take us out of the equation. Why not others?"

"He's going after the key groups," Saxon said. "Covens,

143

wolf packs, vampire clans. If he wipes out the top tier in the beginning, the path will be much smoother for a takeover."

"So we think the darvands are part of this?" Liam asked.

I nodded with enthusiasm. "They're only a test." I pointed a finger at Saxon. "Tell Doran to contact the angels nearby and tell them to stay put. Don't react to any nearby threats."

"What about the demons?" Tate asked. "We're supposed to let them run rampant? Darvands are stupid, but they're still trouble. The humans in that area could be killed."

"I have an idea," I said, although I worried my idea would be met with a slap in the face. Still, I had to try.

Saxon was already on the phone with headquarters, no doubt alerting Doran to the burgeoning crisis.

"Have Emil make the portal and I'll meet you in Anaheim," I said. I bolted for the casino.

"Wait, what…?" Saxon called after me, but there was no time for a discussion. If the demons were already on the attack, then we couldn't afford to lose a single minute.

I streaked through Salt and was relieved that the security guards knew better than to stop me. They seemed to understand that I was permitted to come and go at will, including straight to the boss's office. I wasn't sure how Ingemar would receive my suggestion. It was one thing to rescue Pandora's Pride. It was quite another to help other species in someone else's territory across the country. It wasn't the done thing among supernaturals.

I breezed past the secretary and marched into his private office without knocking. Ingemar was mid-meeting with two vampires. One was dressed in tweed and the other wore a velour tracksuit. They made an interesting combo, to say the least.

"Ingemar, I need you," I announced.

"Miss Wendell, as you can see I'm in a meeting." Ingemar looked ready to eject me from the building via the window.

"This is a crisis," I said. "Whatever's happening here won't matter tomorrow if we don't handle this situation." Okay, maybe a slight exaggeration, but nobody needed to know that.

The tweed vampire turned to observe me. "Sounds important, Ingemar. Maybe we should reschedule."

"Is this your niece?" the velour vampire asked. "She has your coloring."

Ingemar gripped the edge of his desk, the only physical sign of his annoyance. "Miss Wendell is a resident of the casino and our private security consultant."

I placed a hand on the tweed jacket. "I am so sorry to interrupt your meeting, but this really can't wait. Go on now, you two. Off you get."

The two vampires exchanged uncertain glances before vacating the office.

"Call my secretary to reschedule," Ingemar called after them. He shifted his focus to me with narrowed eyes. "There had better be a world-ending, cataclysmic reason for this."

I leaned both hands on the opposite side of the desk. "I need your goons. Now."

"How is it that I have suddenly become *your* security consultant?"

"You like your life, don't you? You'd like to keep it?"

He flinched. "That bad?"

I nodded. "Your guys have the easy part, trust me."

Ingemar pressed a button on the phone. "I need you to issue a Code A."

"Right away, sir," the secretary said.

"They'll be assembled on the rooftop," Ingemar said. "Am I to assume you'll be leading them?"

"If you're okay with that."

Ingemar hesitated. "I can't say this is a moment I ever envisioned for us, but one of the reasons I've survived this long is because I've been willing to adapt when others refused."

"A little flexibility goes a long way." I pushed away from the desk and straightened. "Thank you, Ingemar."

"I suppose I should be thanking you."

"Not yet. Let's wait until this is all over. You can buy me an expensive bottle of booze."

"It will be my pleasure."

I raced from the office and headed to the rooftop where the vampires were starting to congregate. I was pleased to see they'd arrived with weapons in hand. Whatever a Code A was, it seemed to anticipate the need for violence.

I hovered above them, using my wings to sustain my position in midair. "Mr. Halpain asked me to take charge. In a moment, I'll be creating a portal for us. There's a pod of darvands sweeping the city of Anaheim. They're not sharp thinkers. They can be killed in any number of ways, so get creative if you're in the mood but be quick. Humans are off-limits." I paused. "I feel like that should go without saying, but I feel better having said that."

A few of the vampires grunted.

"As I understand it, there's a convention center, a stadium, city hall, and a theme park. Plenty of places for demons to cause trouble," I continued.

One of the bulkier vampires perked up. "A theme park?"

The vampire beside him elbowed him in the ribs. "It's not a vacation, Rupert."

"But you know I can't pass by a rollercoaster without riding it," he complained.

"You can ride the one on the boardwalk when we get back," I said.

"Not the same," Rupert muttered.

"I'll have a portal waiting for you at the end. I appreciate this isn't your usual assignment for Mr. Halpain, but you've been called to a higher purpose and, looking at you now, I think you're all ready to rise to the challenge." In truth, they looked ready to raid a nightclub, but beggars couldn't be choosers.

I lowered myself to the rooftop and set to work on the portal. I felt a tap on my shoulder while I worked.

"What is it?" I asked.

"Do we have to kill them?" a vampire whispered.

I turned to look at him. "The demons?"

He nodded. "I don't mind disarming someone or subduing them, but killing isn't really in my code of ethics."

The vampire worked for a ruthless crime family, yet he was worried about his code of ethics?

I offered a reassuring smile. "I don't care what you do to them, as long as you make sure those demons don't destroy the city." And hopefully the vampires' presence would send a message to Varcin that supernaturals were willing to work together to prevent a takeover. It might not stop him in his tracks, but it might make him slow down and reconsider his plan long enough for us to find him.

The vampire relaxed. "Thank you. I feel much better now."

"Good luck," I told him and turned back to the portal.

The portal creation required complete concentration. It wasn't second nature for me yet the way it was someone like Emil, but I had faith I'd get there. Now that I was fully aware of my abilities and embraced them, everything seemed easier. Magic flowed through me with an intensity I'd never experienced before, even when I wasn't trying to access it. My powers simmered just below the surface, waiting to be called forth and put to use. It felt…good.

Once the portal was ready, I ushered the vampires through in a single-file line. They'd worked themselves into fight mode with chanting and pounding their weapons. It was like watching warriors prepare for the battlefield. I only hoped they all returned. That was one of the challenges of being a leader—I felt responsible for every life I risked. I wondered whether Abra and the others felt that way about the team. It seemed like they did. They had almost a parent-child relationship with the younger members. Of course, in a normal parent-child dynamic, doing as you're told wouldn't kill you.

I jumped through the portal last and emerged in an alley between two buildings. The nearby dumpster reeked of rotting food and I covered my nose and mouth to cut off the stench.

The vampires had already exited the alley and scattered. I rounded the corner and found myself within view of City Hall. Darvand demons were coming out of the woodwork now that the vampires had appeared. The darvands were black two-legged creatures with red eyes and sinewy muscle. Thankfully, the civilians seemed to have the good sense to stay out of their way. The scene reminded me of North Carolina, where the property damage had been the worst part of the attack. I wondered what Varcin had thought of two random supernaturals unexpectedly dispatching the gogome demons he'd sent.

I'd never fought a darvand demon and took a moment to lurk in the shadows and gauge their abilities. They were neither bigger nor faster than the average human. They were, however, stronger. Not stronger than vampires from the Potestas though. I watched with interest as Rupert took on two darvands in front of a fountain. The vampire had muscles the size of bowling balls. He grabbed a darvand in each hand and smashed them into each other. It was like watching two tree trunks fed up with squirrels.

I was so fixated on Rupert that I failed to detect the darvand creeping up on me. He snuck in the first kick, nailing me in the lower back, and I tipped forward. My wings shot out and kept me from falling on my face. I whipped around and released an explosive orb. The darvand didn't move fast enough. Another darvand leaped from the side and shoved me with such force that I went flying across the sidewalk. My cheek slammed into a storefront window and I came face-to-face with a crowd of spectators inside. The woman closest to me gave me an encouraging thumbs up and I rejoined the fight with renewed enthusiasm. Innocent people were relying on me.

The darvand's red eyes seemed to glow with malicious delight. It wiggled its hand, inviting me to attack. I must not have seemed very intimidating.

Big mistake.

I spread my wings and launched myself at the demon. It tried to take cover behind a palm tree, but I hooked my arms and swung around the trunk, landing a solid kick in its chest. The darvand flew backward and crashed into the side of a car.

I turned to get the lay of the land and noticed a woman watching me from one of the storefront windows. Unlike the other window crammed with faces, she stood alone behind the double-wide window. My gaze flicked to the pastel sign hanging over the window. A tea shop called Good Fortune. The woman didn't offer an encouraging thumbs up or even a smile. She simply observed me with a grim expression.

I refocused on the fight and saw that the vampires had herded the darvands into the city center. Music began to play and I recognized the familiar sound of Bach's Brandenburg Concerto No. 5. My father's mage magic had allowed him to conjure music and he'd made good use of it, introducing me to classical music at a young age. In fact, many of my magic lessons had been set to music. I remembered standing across a clearing from my father and listening to this very piece while we sparred.

I returned my attention to the vampires and the darvands. I'd made the right choice asking Ingemar for help. For decades, the vampires had been trained to protect Ingemar's territory. Now they could put their skills to better use and protect all of our territory from Plague demons. It might make the reclusive angels more inclined to open communications with the vampires, something they'd refused to do since the dawn of time.

The battle seemed to culminate in a single inhuman screech. Fangs sank into taut muscle. Bones snapped and cracked. Heads rolled. Darvand heads, specifically.

Once I was confident the darvands were no longer a threat, I sought out the rest of my team. I hadn't spotted any of them during the mayhem. Then again, I'd been somewhat distracted.

"It's under control," Saxon said. "Anaheim is secure."

"No loss of life as far as I know," I said. "Only property damage and some petrified residents."

Liam appeared behind him, wiping the blood from his face with a furry arm. I watched as the thick hair receded and left only his skin visible.

"This is a game of whack-a-demon," the werevamp said. "We can't keep doing this."

"I agree," Saxon said. "It's too reactive. If we're right about these attacks being part of his plan, then we need to stop letting Varcin call the shots."

"I think we should talk to the angels," I said.

"Doran is already with them," Saxon said. "He decided to fill them in on Varcin. See if they knew anything about the demon."

"Let's go find out," I said.

"Are you sure?" Saxon asked.

"You've done more than your part. You don't have to get involved," Saxon said.

I squeezed his hand. "I'm involved, Saxon. Let's go."

We flew north together with me carrying Tate and Saxon carrying Liam, which was more entertaining than it should've been thanks to the werevamp's occasional terrified shouts.

We landed in front of a set of enormous golden gates. Apparently the angels' hub had been a former movie studio before the Plague and already had a solid security infrastructure in place.

Saxon checked his phone. "Doran says to wait out here. There's a discussion with the angelic higher-ups going on now."

Liam examined a tear in his jeans. "You've got to be kidding me. These are brand new."

"Next time don't wear new clothes to a fight," Saxon said.

Liam's head snapped up. "It's not like we had advanced warning."

"What do you think the angels will say?" I asked.

"*Thank you*, if they're smart," Liam shot back.

"This will be the ideal time for Doran to pitch them about banding together," I said. "They'll have to see how crucial it is now."

"They might not be convinced," Saxon said. "We don't have any proof and the fight was thirty miles away."

"Or it might be the best thing that could've happened," Tate said.

Liam looked at her askance. "Lesser demons swarming major players in an effort to destroy them so a Plague demon can advance on the rest of the planet?"

"Think about it," Tate said. "For thirty years, the demons have watched us grow separate and apart from each other and form power clusters instead of a united front. They've already divided us. All they need to do is conquer."

"How many demons do we think Varcin is working with?" I asked.

Tate heaved a sigh. "Anything is possible at this point."

"I'm picturing a pink fairy armadillo militia up next," Liam said.

"These attacks might just be the catalyst that finally brings us all together," I said. "We need to use this to our advantage. Others won't want to be the first target when Varcin decides to enter the final phase of his plan."

"We need to identify all the power centers," Saxon said. "The obvious spots that might be next on Varcin's hit list. He'll likely move faster now that he realizes we're on to him."

"I'm sure Abra has been keeping an updated log," I said. "I need to get back to Anaheim to get the vampires home before they get into trouble. They're like drunken toddlers with fangs."

The hybrid looked at me with warmth simmering in his eyes. "I'll let you know how this pans out."

I offered a hesitant smile. "Thanks."

Liam waved. "See you at home, Callie."

My eyes were still locked on Saxon. "Yes, I'll see you there."

CHAPTER THIRTEEN

ONCE I SENT the vampires through the portal to the rooftop of Salt, I closed it without entering. I wasn't quite ready to return to Atlantica City yet. There was something I wanted to do in Anaheim first.

I walked past a row of palm trees and opened the door to Good Fortune, the tea shop I'd noticed during the brawl. A bell jingled as I entered. The scent of floral perfume and chocolate mingled in the air. No one inside seemed concerned about the chaos that had taken place outside. The room was filled with well-dressed customers engaged in polite conversation over pots of tea and delectable baked goods.

"Kind of fancy for a tea shop," I said to myself. It was a far cry from the establishments in Atlantica City.

"People here want to be reminded of a more civilized time," a woman said. She wore a red dress with a string of black pearls around her neck.

"There was a woman here earlier," I said. "She stood in the window during the fight. She looked like you." Only she hadn't been wearing a red dress.

"That would be my twin sister, Esther. I'm Elmira," she said, offering her hand. "Welcome to our shop."

"Nice to meet you. I'm Callie."

She cocked her head, studying me. "You're more than Callie, though, aren't you?"

"It's a nickname."

Elmira wagged a finger at me. "No need to be evasive. I'll uncover your secrets." She snapped a finger. "I hear a bird singing a sad song."

I flinched.

"A lark," she said, triumphant.

"Another nickname," I said stiffly. I didn't come here to unearth my past. I was well-acquainted with it now. It was only the future I was keen to glimpse.

"You've gone by another name as well," Elmira said.

"I have, but that's not why I'm here."

She smiled. "Well, I don't think it's for tea. You reek of urgency."

"The urgency has passed," I said. "You might've heard the ruckus."

"Not really. We played classical music. Loudly."

I cracked a smile. "Oh, that was you. I could hear it, but I wasn't sure where it came from."

"I hope it wasn't too distracting during the fight. We were only trying to distract everyone from the danger outside."

I shook my head. "It was a genius move."

Elmira cast a sweeping glance across the room. "There's a quiet table in the corner where we can talk. Have a seat and I'll join you in a minute."

"Is your sister here?" I wasn't sure why I wanted to see her. I just felt compelled and I'd learned to trust that instinct.

"She went to rest upstairs after the scuffle. We have a small apartment above the shop."

"I'd like to speak to her, if she's awake."

Elmira studied me for a long moment. "I'll see if she's available, shall I?"

I threaded my way through the tables until I reached a table for two at the back. It was set apart from the other tables and I assumed it was reserved for Elmira's business transactions.

Elmira joined me a few minutes later with a tray. "My sister will be with us shortly. Thought you might like a drink while we get acquainted."

She set the tray between us and I noticed a packet of cards beside the pot, nestled between two cups and saucers.

"That's probably a good idea." I'd worked up quite a hunger and thirst during the fight.

"You're accustomed to denying your needs," Elmira said, more of a statement than a question.

"Easy to deny them when you don't know what they are," I said.

"Is that what brings you to my shop?" Elmira asked.

"Another lady read my tea leaves recently and I'd like to see whether I get a similar reading from you."

She arched an eyebrow. "Not quite a believer?"

"My father used to say a second opinion is always a good idea," I said. That was a lie, of course. My father discouraged me from seeking answers from external sources because he was worried I'd uncover the truth. If he hadn't died, I'd still be living in ignorance while the world was under siege.

"Your father sounds like a wise man," Elmira said.

"He had his moments. Anyway, I'd like more information about my future and I can't go back to the original source right now."

She shuffled the cards. "You haven't killed her, have you?"

Laughter escaped me. "Of course not."

"Ah, well. You can never be too sure. Some folks get very testy about their futures, especially when they receive news they don't want to hear." She cut the deck and shuffled again. "Would you prefer leaves again or are you open to other types of readings?"

"This is a tea shop. I assumed tea leaves were on the menu."

"They are, but my sister and I prefer cards."

I watched as she split the deck in half in front of me. "I don't mind." Given my current home was a casino, cards seemed appropriate.

"Choose a card, my dear."

I gaped at them. "These aren't tarot cards. These are for poker."

"And?"

I shook my head. "Is this going to work?"

She leaned against the chair and regarded me. "You've charmed an object or two, I imagine."

"I have."

"Then you should know as well as anyone that the object is simply that—a conduit to perform whatever magic you possess. I don't need a tarot card to read you. In fact, I don't even need a card, but it makes the whole process more enjoyable."

She was right. I'd enchanted a poker chip, a playing card —the item wasn't as important as the spell it contained.

"Okay, you've convinced me," I said.

Elmira continued removing the cards from the packet. "This lady who read you before. Was she a mage?"

"A witch."

"Thought as much." She poured the tea into both cups.

"What gave it away?"

"You." She eyed me closely. "You wanted a second opinion, but you wanted it from a different sect. Mages are the next best thing to witches, are we not?"

"My father was a mage," I said, "but he wasn't a diviner."

"Not many men are." Elmira removed the tray and pot from the table and left them on the floor against the wall. "Just need a bit of space."

"I'll take it from here, dear sister."

I glanced up to see the woman from the window. Esther. The women were clearly fraternal twins. They shared the same coloring and their bodies had a similar slender build, but the similarities ended there. Where Elmira had large eyes and a slightly upturned nose, Esther's eyes were smaller and closer together and her nose was straight and serious.

Elmira cut a quick glance at her twin. "Are you certain? I don't mind if you're tired."

Esther dragged over a chair from a neighboring table. "I'm not too tired for this."

"I saw you in the window," I said. "You didn't look very happy."

"Neither would you if demons had invaded your hometown," Esther snapped.

"Esther, my love, we should be thanking this young woman for her service. After all, she brought the vampires to fight them."

"I fought, too," Esther said.

Realization swept over me. "You were performing a spell from the window."

"Wasn't much, but I did what I could," she said gruffly.

I felt strangely moved by her admission. I got the distinct impression that Esther didn't go out of her way for others very often. "Thank you," I said.

"Anything to get rid of those blood-suckers," Esther said.

"You have something against vampires?" I asked.

"They don't belong here," she said simply.

"But you prefer them to demons, I imagine," I said.

"Lesser of two evils." Esther pushed the two piles closer to me and fanned them out across the table. "Just one to start with. There's no right or wrong."

I didn't stop to think. I simply chose one from the middle and flipped it over. Ace of spades.

Elmira looked eagerly at my selection but gave nothing away.

"And another," Esther said.

I slipped a card from the lineup and turned it over. Ace of hearts. I tried to gauge the Elmira's reaction, but she was careful to keep her expression neutral.

"And now a third," Esther said.

I chose from the far end this time and set the card beside the other two choices. Queen of Clubs.

"Hmm. Critical paths," she said.

My gaze shifted from the cards to her face. "How many?"

She frowned at the cards. "Three, I'd say."

Three again.

"Each one involves sacrifice," Esther continued.

"Did the witch tell you all this?" Elmira asked, curious.

"Some of it," I admitted. "Though she left out the part about sacrifice."

"Probably didn't want to upset you," Esther scoffed. "You must've known her."

"Not well," I said.

She flicked a glance at me. "But she liked you. That's a mistake. Nothing should influence the reading."

"So three paths lie ahead. Got it," I said, not wanting to discuss Marie.

"No, you misunderstand me," Esther said. "You had three paths, but the choices have already been made."

"Wait. I don't have to choose between three paths?" I asked. I assumed it was a choice between three paths, not that I would make three choices.

"No," Esther said. "The three paths you chose will determine the outcome."

"And you're sure I've already made the choices?" I asked.

Elmira peered over her sister's shoulder. "Yes, I see that. The wheels are already in motion."

My heart stuttered. "When?" How could I have made such monumental decisions without realizing it?

Esther scowled. "Did you expect a flashing neon sign or the trumpets of angels?"

"I just assumed if it was that important, it would be obvious."

"Sometimes the most important things in life are the ones we barely notice. The whisper of the wind. The turning of the leaves. The pitter patter of falling rain." Esther swept the cards toward her and reformed a single pile. "Do you notice every sunrise? And yet it signals that we've arrived at another day. Pretty important, wouldn't you agree?"

I struggled to come up with a recent moment where I'd been presented with three choices. "Which paths did I choose?" I looked at her, my heart pounding. "How will I know whether I chose the right ones?"

Esther shrugged. "When it all works out."

Gods above, it was the fate of the world, not a blossoming relationship.

I sat for a lingering moment, running through events since I'd left Salem. I'd intended to go to Florida to see the angels, but instead I chose to return to Atlantica City when I realized the Pride was in trouble. Then I chose to go to the pocket realm and rescue them. And then...

I chose to come here, to continue to work with the supernaturals who betrayed me.

I dug a handful of bills from my pocket and set them on the table. "Thank you." I jumped from my chair so quickly that I nearly knocked it over.

"There's one more thing you should know," Esther said.

I stopped to look at her. "What is it?"

She tapped the card face up on the table. "Sometimes you must destroy in order to create."

A lump formed in my throat at the possible meaning. "I'll take it under advisement, thanks."

I was shaking when I left Good Fortune, reliving recent events. I'd definitely made three choices. The question is—were they the right ones?

CHAPTER FOURTEEN

I RETURNED to my room from Anaheim, leaving the rest of
the team to handle the debriefing at headquarters. I had no
interest in being a part of that. I did, however, agree that I
would check with Renee for an update tonight. Apparently,
Doran wasn't enthusiastic about seeing her again and had
asked that I handle the dream walking, despite the fae's will-
ingness to help. I found it ironic that the senior members of
the Pride were taking Renee's betrayal so hard given what
they'd done to us.

I was famished by the time my friends returned to Salt, so
we ordered room service and had our own team meeting to
discuss Varcin.

"We did learn a few things during our stay in the Plaza de
Pocket Dimension," Liam said. He'd inhaled an entire
double-cheeseburger before I managed to finish a single fish
taco.

"Like what?" I asked. "You prefer dry heat to humidity?"

"That Purvis snores louder then Liam," Tate said. "Who
knew?"

Liam wore a sheepish expression. "I didn't say we learned anything good."

"Varcin's got to be ready to launch his full-scale attack soon," Saxon said. "He won't want to give us too much time to find him."

"You don't think he'll change course now that you're back in action?" I asked.

"Not if these demon attacks are any indication," Saxon said. "I think he intends to go ahead with whatever the original plan was and take his chances with us."

"He certainly seems to have convinced an army of nuisance demons to do the grunt work before the main event," Tate said. She sucked down a glass of iced tea.

I shuddered to contemplate what that main event would be.

"If you think about it, our abduction was basically a coup," Tate said. "If I were Varcin, I'd want to get rid of any centralized source of power first. Starting with Pandora's Pride was a no-brainer."

I swallowed the last of my tacos. "So what next?"

"We need to anticipate his next move and beat him to it," Tate said.

"If we can find out where he's operating from, then we can storm his headquarters," Saxon said.

"Yeah, see how he likes it," Liam said.

Saxon shot him a silencing look. "Then we can shut down whatever he has planned before it happens."

"Any leads on his lair from Nita?" I asked.

Liam chewed on a fry. "Yeah, it's totally a lair. Why are we calling it his headquarters? It makes him sound official."

"He was holed up in a pocket realm for centuries," I said. "The demon isn't going to be picky about his location."

"He might be if he needs access to ley lines or some other source of magical power," Tate countered.

"Wherever he is, we know he's in this realm," Saxon said. "He didn't step foot in the pocket realm when we were there."

"Can't say I blame him," Liam said. "I'd avoid it like the... plague." He scratched his chin thoughtfully. "Can a Plague demon avoid something like the plague? That's a far more complicated statement than I anticipated. Borders on philosophical."

Tate blew out an exasperated breath. "Borders on ridiculous."

I wiped my mouth with my napkin to get rid of the chipotle sauce. "Hopefully, Renee will have news for us and we'll finally have the advantage."

"That dream walking comes in handy," Liam said. "I wish they'd given me a few angel traits."

"Not for lack of effort," I said.

The werevamp studied me. "Do you feel new and improved now that you can access all your traits?"

I shrugged. "I don't know. I still feel like me, just with a greater sense of responsibility."

"What do you think your father would say about you being here as part of the Pride?" Liam asked. "Especially after all he went through to keep you away."

Saxon elbowed him hard in the ribs. "Enough with the interrogation."

"It's okay, Saxon. I can answer." I looked at Liam. "Honestly, I think he would understand. He did his part. He raised me independently of the Pride. Kept me safe. Who knows what I'd be like if I'd grown up here?"

"Worse than Evadne, I bet," Liam muttered.

"Anyway, the point is I'm choosing to be here now," I said. "I wasn't given that choice before and neither were you."

Saxon finished his last piece of steak. "For what it's worth, I'm glad we're all together now." His gaze lingered on me and I felt a rush of warmth flow through me.

"I should get ready for bed," I said. "The sooner I touch base with Renee, the sooner we might be able to find Varcin."

"In that case, we'll take our party next door," Liam offered.

"No party for me," Tate said. "I'm exhausted."

I left them to clean up while I showered and dressed for bed. Once I tuned out the sound of Liam's voice in the adjoining room, I was able to focus on Renee and drift off to sleep.

I opened my eyes to find myself blanketed in darkness. A shiver ran down the length of my spine and I woke up with a start.

"Callie?" Tate murmured. "What is it?"

"Something's wrong," I said. I shot out of bed and hunted for my shoes.

Tate pulled herself into a seated position and wiped the sleep from her eyes. "Where are you going?"

"To Wilmington." I slipped on my shoes, my heart racing.

"Take Saxon. Don't go alone."

She was right. What if this was some kind of trap? I burst through the adjacent doorway and nudged Saxon.

"Wake up," I said in a stage whisper.

Saxon stirred and opened his eyes. "Is everything okay?"

I shook my head. "We need to fly to Wilmington."

He didn't ask any more questions. He was out of bed in a flash, pulling on clothes and shoes. We left from my window and Tate closed it behind us.

We flew in darkness over the shoreline, neither one of us speaking. It was partly drowsiness and partly impending fear. The feeling I'd experienced in the dream could only be described as emptiness. Although it was possible I'd simply failed to make a connection, I knew in the pit of my stomach that something bad had happened to Renee.

The door to her apartment was ajar. I rushed inside and

found the fae in bed. Bloodstains seeped through the sheets. Like Willem Dougherty, her throat had been slashed. Her eyes were pinned on the ceiling, unblinking.

I kneeled beside her and tried to steady my breathing. Tears pricked my eyes. I felt a hand on my shoulder and craned my neck to look at Saxon. His expression was grim.

"We did this to her," I whispered. "We shouldn't have put her in such a difficult position."

"We didn't do this to her, Callie. Varcin did."

I turned back to Renee. "Do you think he killed the daughter, too?"

"No idea." Saxon crouched beside the body. "We don't even know if Varcin did this himself or if he sent someone."

"What kind of monster murders a woman in her sleep?" I asked.

"A Plague demon."

I turned to look at him with tears spilling down my cheeks. Renee didn't deserve to die like this. She was only trying to save her daughter.

"We have to stop him, Saxon."

His jaw tensed. "And we will."

We reconvened the next morning in the conference room at headquarters to update everyone on Renee's fate and hear the results of Nita's research.

"We need to find the daughter," Natasha said. "She could be our link to finding Varcin."

"She's been missing for months," Saxon said. "The trail will be too cold."

Nita stood at the front of the room with her whiteboard. "I can tell you what I've learned about Varcin so far. Maybe something will help."

Abra offered a nod of approval. "It's time to pursue another path."

"This is our friend, Varcin," Nita said. An image of a demon appeared on the whiteboard. He looked like a humanoid tree with sinewy muscles the color of oak that stretched the length of his body. The muscles twisted and bulged like roots and branches. Two black pools served as eyes and two sharp teeth curved over his upper lip.

"I didn't realize ugly could be a superpower," Liam said.

Nita ignored him. "Varcin is hostile to humans. Before he was imprisoned by the gods, he murdered entire villages out of pure malice."

"Yes, he's hostile. I think we've established that. Something more useful, maybe?" Natasha prompted.

"What are his strengths and weaknesses?" Saxon asked.

"Physical strength seems to be his primary power, along with intelligence," Nita said. "He has a history of finding lesser demons to fill in any gaps for powers he doesn't possess."

"Or fae," Natasha said with a trace of bitterness.

Instinctively, I glanced away. I was arguably the living embodiment of that same idea.

"He's also a demon of droughts," Nita continued.

Liam shook his head ruefully. "Man, I've been there, but all it takes is one good date to turn things around."

Nita glowered at him. "He's most likely in a dry climate."

"One of the deserts?" Tate asked. "Plenty of space to gather his demon friends for a purge the world party."

I contemplated the suggestion. "I don't know. If you're a big, bad demon of droughts, wouldn't you rather cause them?"

"So you think his hideout might be somewhere in the U.K.?" Liam asked.

"Or somewhere there's moisture in the air even when it's not raining," I said.

"I can research for unusual activity," Nita offered. "If Callie's right about the desire to suck all the moisture out of the air, that should be easy to spot."

"Bring up a current map," Abra commanded.

Nita tapped the whiteboard and a map of the world appeared.

"We won't be able to see anything with that view," Emil said. "Focus on one quadrant at a time."

I didn't even know what to look for. I only saw patches of green, brown, and blue.

"Belize," Nita said, pointing. "There's something happening in Belize."

"Something as in a drunken orgy or something as in a Plague demon summit?" Liam asked. "I know which answer I'd prefer."

Nita enlarged the image so it was easier to see. "There's an old Mayan temple on a ridge above the Mopan River. It's close to the border of Guatemala."

"What makes you think Varcin is there?" Saxon asked. "There are lots of temples in that region."

Nita couldn't resist an excited smile. "Because the Mopan River should be right there." She tapped a thin brown line. "According to the map, it's currently thirty miles of dirt."

"Which Mayan temple is there?" Doran asked.

Tate snapped her fingers. "El Castillo."

"Of course." Abra nodded. "That makes sense. Axis mundi."

Liam glanced between grandmother and granddaughter. "Care to share with the class?"

"What's axis mundi?" Saxon asked.

"The center of the celestial world," Nita explained. "It's

the best place to access another realm because it's where the higher and lower realms connect."

"There's even a frieze on the temple that depicts the tree of life," Tate said. "I studied it in art class a few years ago."

"Why would he care about connecting to other realms if he only wants to wipe out civilization?" I asked.

"He's probably not using it for access to the realms," Nita said. "More likely he's using it as a power source, or planning to."

"Then we need to get there before he leaves," Saxon said. "Stop whatever he has planned."

"Yggdrasil," I said, an idea forming. "The Norse's Nine Worlds are connected by Yggdrasil and they used the branches of the tree to access the other realms."

Doran cast a quizzical eye at me. "You want to use Odin's tree? Why?"

I shook my head in an effort to clear the tangle of thoughts. "Not Yggdrasil specifically. The concept. That was also an axis mundi." I pointed at the whiteboard. "A connection between realms. A way to funnel the demon and his friends from this one into another one."

"We could use his own lair against him," Saxon said.

Nita's eyes shone with excitement. "Yes!"

"But there's no actual tree there," Purvis said. "It's a frieze."

"The axis mundi is already there," I said. "We'll plant our own."

Liam licked his lips. "Um, Callie. You do know trees take quite a long time to grow, right? That Norse tree is centuries old and, I may be wrong, but I don't think we have that kind of time."

"For once, you're not wrong," Saxon said.

"It's called magic, Liam," Tate said.

"We'll use the axis mundi point to funnel Varcin and his

friends into the pocket realm, and then we'll do what the gods should've done." I paused for effect. "We'll destroy it."

"Can we do that?" Tate asked.

"We have to try." It was the only way to make sure the demons never returned. If the pocket dimension ceased to exist, then so did they.

"Callie's right," Saxon said. "This is our best option."

"What about the other Plague demons?" Emil asked. "If you destroy the pocket realm, we lose all hope of ever sending the rest back to it."

Nita jumped up and down, giddy. "This is brilliant. We can take care of every Plague demon in one fell swoop."

Liam laughed. "Oh, sure. We'll just ask all the demons in the world to swing by for a special ritual. Someone prepare the embossed invitations."

Nita changed the image on the whiteboard to a world tree. "They don't need to be present as long as we have one physical link, the more powerful, the better. We'll harness the power of axis mundi and the world tree to do the rest."

"As much as I like this idea, I don't think we should risk staging it at Varcin's temple," Abra said. "We have no idea what kind of rituals he may have already performed there. We need a clean space that we claim as our own."

Nita turned back to the whiteboard. "We can choose another axis mundi." She tapped the screen and enlarged the map of North America. "There."

I squinted to see where her finger pointed. "Arizona?"

"Sedona, to be exact," Nita said, twirling back to face us.

"If we set up at a different location, it'll give us time to have everything ready. All we'll need is Varcin," Saxon said.

"Gee, because it'll be so simple to abduct him from his stronghold guarded by all his demon buddies," Liam said.

"To create our own access point to the pocket realm, our own world tree..." Abra touched the strand of pearls around her neck, thinking. "That will take more magic than we're capable of on our own. We are talking about the kind of power that has never been harnessed by anyone lesser than a god."

"How can we access that kind of power?" Tate asked.

I slapped my hands on the table. "The Sunstone. We can use the Sunstone."

Everyone exchanged uneasy glances at the mention of the gemstone.

"If we use the stone for that spell, it will be lost to us forever," Abra said.

Doran placed a gentle hand on her shoulder. "But if the spell is successful, we'll have no more need of it."

"Will it be enough?" Natasha asked.

"We can get help," I said.

Abra clucked her tongue. "What makes you think anyone will help us, child? We've worked alone for decades for a reason."

"This isn't about us, Abra," I said. "This is about the fate of the world."

"My dear girl, this has always been about the fate of the world," Abra replied.

I thought about those I'd met since leaving the Rocky Mountains. Ogres, witches, vampires...

"We need to build a coalition. Gather as much magic as we can get."

Tate raised a hand. "I'll go to Wayzata and speak to the witches there. They're one of the most powerful covens in the Midwest and they helped us once before. They might be willing to do it again."

"You could go to California," I told Doran. "Ask the angels there to get involved now that we have a concrete plan."

"We'll need the fae," Saxon said.

Emil shook his head. "They will be resistant."

"Then show them the alternative," I shot back. "Show them the future that awaits them if they refuse to cooperate." With their potent magic, the inclusion of the fae was critical to our success.

"We begged for their help after the Plague and they cast us out," Purvis said. "What makes you think they'll join us now?"

"That was thirty years ago," I said. "Any fool can see that the world has gotten worse instead of better. Thirty years ago, they still had hope that things would go back to normal. That the demons would be nothing but a blip in their reality. But the demons are still here."

Purvis nodded thoughtfully. "Wolves have no magic to offer, but they might be willing to lend their best fighters to take down Varcin. I suspect there will be plenty of demons to keep at bay."

"Abra, you should go to Salem," I said. "Talk to Marie. I've already laid the groundwork. The rest is up to you."

"Yes, I believe you're right."

My brow lifted. "You do?" I'd expected more resistance from Abra.

"You must understand, Calandra. We've been on a straight path for thirty years with no reason to deviate."

"And now?"

"You've shown us another way forward." The witch lowered her gaze. "Despite everything, I am not the monster you want me to be."

"And I'm exactly the monster you wanted me to be. Funny how that turned out."

"You're not a monster, Callie," Natasha said.

I laughed. "Oh, no? How would you describe me then?"

The vampire wore a sad smile. "That's easy. You're the best of all of us."

CHAPTER FIFTEEN

"This is Iowa, huh?" I surveyed the trees around us. "Based on your description, Liam, I expected more corn."

The portal had spit us into a forest of silver maples and majestic bur oaks. The air smelled fresh and crisp, not quite as fresh as the mountains but certainly more so than Atlantica City.

"I didn't think there were any trees in Iowa," Liam remarked.

"Iowa has over a billion trees," Purvis said. "Something you'd know if you'd paid attention in geography class when you were younger."

"I hope Tate has good luck with the Wayzata witches," Saxon said.

I stepped gingerly over a fallen tree. "I'm more concerned about Abra in Massachusetts. That one could go either way."

Nathaniel and Lloyd had volunteered to accompany Abra to Massachusetts. As powerful as the older witch was, she was out of practice when it came to trouble in the field and we couldn't risk her safety. For better or worse, she was essential to completion of the spell. Without Abra, our whole plan was doomed.

Purvis stopped abruptly and crouched low, signaling for us to follow suit. A werewolf emerged from behind one of the larger oaks. He was burly and bald, an unexpected look for a werewolf. I wondered whether he had bald patches in his coat when he shifted.

"You'll want to think twice before you step over that border," the werewolf warned.

Liam pointed to the ground between us. "That line there? Is that the border?"

A low growl rumbled from the werewolf.

Liam rolled his eyes. "Oh, please. I'm one of you. I can make the same sound." He mimicked the werewolf's low growl.

The werewolf spat on the ground. "You are most definitely *not* one of us. You have fangs and you smell like death warmed over."

Liam produced two hairy arms. "I beg to differ."

The werewolf gaped at the set of arms, uncertain how to process this partial shift. "That's...not possible," he said. "My oldest brother is the alpha of this pack and even he can't perform such feats."

"Your oldest brother?" Purvis echoed. He sauntered closer to the border wolf. "Knox?"

The werewolf stared back at him, appearing to see him for the first time. "Purvis? Is that really you? I thought I caught a familiar scent, but there are so many strange smells in this group." He crossed the invisible line to engulf the older werewolf in a warm embrace. "Been such a long time. Thought you might be dead."

Purvis thumped him once on the back before releasing him. "No such luck."

"How's the family? Is that nephew of yours here?" Knox

craned his neck to examine us. "That little guy was always hot on your heels."

Purvis's expression darkened. "I'm afraid Leto is no longer with us."

Knox winced at the news. "I'm sorry to hear that. He was a fine boy." He waved a hand in our direction. "Why would you lead outsiders to our territory? The alpha's not gonna be pleased."

"He won't be pleased no matter what." Purvis's smile failed to reach his eyes.

"Well, you know the process, Purvis," Knox said. "If you want a meeting, you need to wait here and I'll let…"

"No," I interjected. "We don't have time for pack protocol. We need to see the alpha now."

Knox raised his brow and gave me an appraising look. "You smell worse than that one." He motioned to Liam. "What's your deal, sweetheart?"

Saxon pushed his way past us and stepped directly in front of Knox. "Her deal, *sweetheart*, is that we're here to save your lives and we don't have the luxury of time."

Knox snarled. "You might want to take a few steps back. Werewolves are pretty protective of their personal space. I would think you'd know that if you've spent enough time around that one." He inclined his head toward Purvis.

Saxon snapped his fangs before taking a single step backward.

"What's all this about?" Knox asked. His tone was a bit more receptive now, despite the posturing.

"Take us to the alpha," I said. "Please."

Knox looked me up and down before turning to Purvis. "You're going to let them disrespect me like that?"

Purvis sighed. "They're not trying to be disrespectful. They're young and foolish and trying to press the urgency of the matter with the limited interpersonal skills that they have."

I cast a sideways glance at Purvis. "Gee, thanks."

Knox glanced at each of us, seeming to contemplate his options. Finally, he pointed to Purvis. "Just you. This is were-wolf-only turf and I'm not about to get my ass handed to me because I disobeyed orders."

Liam groaned loudly. "And this is why you're under threat, you insular…"

"That's enough," Saxon said sternly.

Purvis touched my arm. "Her, too."

Knox's eyes narrowed. "I don't see…"

"And you won't see, but I'm telling you I need her there," Purvis said. "Believe me, I wouldn't be here at all if it weren't absolutely necessary."

Knox gave a reluctant nod. "Don't think about following us," he advised the others. "We've got eyes in the trees, too." He pointed to the trees surrounding us.

Liam held up his hands in acquiescence. "We'll be on our best behavior, playing tic-tac-toe with sticks in the dirt."

We accompanied Knox to a cluster of log cabins in the middle of the forest. Each one appeared to be the same size so it was impossible to know which one belonged to the alpha. I suspected that was by design.

We received several curious glances from the werewolves we passed, but no one questioned our presence. Knox's presence seemed to be enough to keep them at bay.

He knocked on the front door and waited with his head bowed. The door cracked open and he exchanged quiet words with whomever answered it.

Knox turned to us. "This is where I leave you. It was good to see you again, old friend."

Purvis nodded. "Same. Try not to give the young ones a

hard time back there or you might find yourself in deeper trouble than you expect."

Knox's lip curled slightly. "Appreciate the tip."

The door opened fully and Purvis entered first. I stayed close behind, not wanting to risk getting locked out of the conversation. I wasn't sure why Purvis had insisted on bringing me, but I knew he must've had a good reason. If there was one thing I'd learned about the senior members of the Pride, it was that they didn't do anything without a good reason.

A middle-aged werewolf greeted us in the open-plan living room. "Purvis, how wonderful to see you again." She clasped his hands and kissed his cheek.

"Selma. You look as beautiful as ever." He angled his head toward me. "This is one of my companions, Callie Wendell."

"Lovely to meet you." She gave me a curious look before returning her attention to Purvis. "I never thought we'd see you again."

Purvis shrugged. "These are desperate times."

"Yes, you always did have a gloomy outlook, didn't you?" Selma asked, not unkindly.

"Can't say I was wrong."

"Trent is in his office," Selma said. "Can I offer you any refreshments? We're well-stocked with beer."

"No thanks. We're on a time-sensitive mission." Purvis relaxed slightly. "But we appreciate the offer."

I sensed tension between them and wondered whether there was more to their story. I knew so little about the history of Purvis and the others. They kept their own pasts as secret as they'd kept mine.

Selma delivered us to the alpha's office. "Visitors, darling. Looks very official."

Trent glanced up from the paperwork on his desk. "If anyone would've told me that being the alpha of a werewolf pack meant so much bookkeeping and paperwork, I might've refused the title." His expression changed when he spotted Purvis and I couldn't decide whether he was going to smile or scowl.

"Good to see you again, Trent," Purvis said.

The werewolf rose to his feet. He was a good six inches taller than Purvis with muscular arms and a broad chest. His long, reddish-brown hair looked like a mane, which must've irked his younger, follicly-challenged brother.

"I can't decide whether to hug you or punch you," Trent said.

Well, at least he was honest.

Purvis offered his hand and Trent came out from behind the desk to pull him into a bear hug.

"Something bad must be after you to bring you back here," Trent said. "Can't think of any other reason you'd step foot on my turf."

"Not after me. After all of us. A major threat."

Trent laughed and shook his head. "Still catching Plague demons, are we?" He cut a quick glance at me. "And who's this? Your assistant?"

"Callie Wendell," I said.

He sniffed the air between us. "Smells like you've been mixing with a lot of supernaturals. I can't detect your scent, but I smell wolf."

"She *is* a lot of supernaturals," Purvis said.

I stiffened. So this was the reason Purvis wanted to bring me. This was a dog-and-pony show and I was the star pony.

Trent peered at me. "I don't understand."

"I'm part werewolf. Part fae. Witch. Angel. Vampire. A supernatural potpourri."

He stared at me, seeming to process my revelation. "I don't believe you. That isn't possible."

"She was designed to be a weapon in the fight against

Plague demons," Purvis said. "This is the length we were willing to go to for the sake of this realm. We took an innocent child…" He stopped and rubbed the spot between his eyebrows. "We took innocent children, gave them more power than they otherwise would have, and turned them into professional fighters." The note of regret in his voice was unmistakable.

"And now?" Trent asked.

"We think we've found another way to defeat the demons and I very much hope it works because I never want to repeat this experiment again."

I looked at Purvis. "Do you mean that?"

His brown eyes softened. "I can't speak for the others, but I certainly do. Seeing what this has done to you, to Liam. Evadne." He swallowed hard. "Even Leto. The one thing I never intended was to hurt my own kin and yet that's exactly what I've done."

Trent looked at Purvis with interest. "Sounds like we've both made some mistakes these past thirty years." He returned to the spot behind his desk but remained standing. "And how does my pack play into whatever this is?"

"There's a Plague demon…" Purvis began.

Trent groaned. "There've been Plague demons for thirty years, Purvis, yet we've not only survived, we've flourished."

"Because you've hidden away here in a protective bubble," Purvis said.

"And what's wrong with that?" Trent asked. "My responsibility is to the pack, not the wider world."

"This Plague demon might change your mind," Purvis said.

"And why is that?" The alpha examined him closely.

"Varcin is smarter," Purvis said. "He's been biding his time. Watching how the world turned. Gathering intel until he was ready to strike."

"And what?" Trent asked. "You're telling me he plans to strike here? Nobody would dare launch an attack on us. We'll wipe the forest floor with their carcasses."

"He's been testing boundaries, mobilizing nuisance demons to see whether he can draw out the power centers. He sent demons not far from here a few weeks ago, to see whether you or the fae would respond to the threat."

"We heard about it, but we didn't see a need to intervene," Trent said.

"His plan is to eliminate the biggest threats before he comes marching in and planting his flag," Purvis said. "One of these times, it's going to be more than a drill. We want to get to him before that happens."

"Not only that, if we get to Varcin now," I began, "we have a shot at eliminating *all* Plague demons."

Trent scratched his mane, appearing intrigued. "All of 'em?"

I nodded. "We have a plan."

"And where is this Varcin now?" Trent asked.

"We have reason to believe he's in Belize," I said.

"If you know this, then why are you here instead of there?" he asked.

"Because we need to gather more power first," I said. "Our plan requires more than just our organization. It seems to me that we all have a vested interest in stopping Varcin and wiping demons from the plane of existence."

"And you'd like our help," Trent said matter-of-factly.

"We need muscle to handle the nuisance demons," Purvis said.

"We'll take care of Varcin, but we need to be able to get to him without interruption," I said. "That means clearing the path of his minions."

"I have a responsibility to the pack," Trent said. "I can't

send my wolves to another country to fight demons that haven't shown themselves to be a direct threat."

"If we don't fight them there, trust me, we'll be fighting them right here soon enough," I said.

"Then I leave my own territory vulnerable to attack," Trent said. He frowned at Purvis. "You can't expect me to put the lives of others above those of my pack."

"I have a suggestion," I said, "but you're not going to like it."

Trent eyed me curiously. "Well, that's one way to sell it."

"The closest supernatural hub to you belongs to the fae," I said. "Form an alliance with them. Make a deal to protect each other's lands in case of an attack."

"You want me to ask the fae for help defending my own land?" He clutched his stomach and laughed heartily. "We've managed on our own for decades. We don't need the fae or anybody else."

Purvis approached the desk. "Do you think I'd be here if it weren't absolutely necessary? Do you think I want to see *her* here with you?"

Trent's face flickered with something bordering on pity. "No." He drummed his fingers on the desk. "Have you spoken with the queen yet?"

"We have some of our members there now," Purvis said.

He dragged a hand through his mane. "How many wolves do you need?"

"As many as you can spare," Purvis said. "When the time comes, we'll send a portal for them."

"How soon?" Trent asked.

"As soon as we're ready to go," I said.

Trent hesitated, his features flickering with indecision. Finally, he nodded. "Then my wolves will be ready. Tell the queen I'll be in touch."

Elation rushed through me. "Thank you. You won't regret it."

"I sure hope not," Trent said. "Because, believe me, you don't want to be on the wrong side of the pack."

I rode a high all the way back to the group. The promise of werewolves was a huge win for us. I hoped everyone else was having similar luck.

We met Emil and Natasha at the neighboring territory where the fae compound was located. The two of them were brought to see the queen while the rest of us waited. If we managed to connect the pack and the fae for this one endeavor, maybe it would open the door to future involvement, assuming there was a future.

"Fae can be kind of fickle," Liam said. "They may not believe us."

"Then Emil had best put on his most convincing face," Saxon said.

"Ah, the one he wore when he threatened us with punishment when we were teenagers." Liam did an imitation of Emil that made Saxon laugh and the sound was music to my ears.

"That face worked on you, did it?" I asked him skeptically.

"Everyone except Evadne," Saxon said. "Nothing worked on her, but it scared the rest of us into submission."

"Speak of the devil and she shall appear."

I whirled around to see Evadne standing behind us, hands on hips, with half a dozen weapons strapped to her back.

"Holy hell," Liam breathed.

"How did you find us?" I asked.

"Nita, how else?" She strode forward to join the group.

"And your portal actually got you here?" Liam asked.

Evadne scowled at him. "I'd use one of my weapons on you, but I'm saving them for more important targets."

Purvis welcomed her with a warm handshake. "Welcome back, Evadne."

"I don't know that I'm *back*," she said. "I'm just here."

"How was Vegas?" I asked.

"Noisy and crowded." She touched the bark of a nearby tree. "It was time to take a break. Find peace and tranquility in the forest."

Liam smirked. "You got kicked out, didn't you?"

Evadne raised her chin. "Apparently, they don't like when you create portals by the roulette wheel because you're too drunk to walk back to your room."

"They kicked you out of Vegas for that?" Saxon asked. "Seems harsh."

Evadne bit her lip. "I may have been so drunk that I accidentally teleported a few of their customers to Phoenix instead. It turned out to be a headache for the pit boss."

Saxon clapped her on the shoulder, grinning. "It's okay to miss us, you know. We missed you, too."

"And it looks like you brought back some gifts for the rest of us," Liam said, eyeing her weapons.

"These are my winnings. They pretty much let you bet with anything there." Evadne nodded toward the wall of the compound. "Are we going to ring the bell or stand out here yammering?"

"Emil and Natasha are already in there," Saxon said.

"I feel like I'm at the kiddie table at Christmas dinner," Liam complained.

"It's better this way," Purvis said. "The more voices in there, the less likely we are to keep the conversation on track. The fae can be a pain in the ass and we need their support."

Liam laughed. "Now I see where Evadne gets it."

Evadne clocked him so hard, he staggered backward.

The ground shook and Liam looked around warily. "She didn't hit me *that* hard."

Purvis inhaled the scents of the forest. "Something's coming."

"Something like a cart carrying roasted chestnuts?" Liam asked. "Because I could go for a snack."

A shadow passed over the werewolf's features. "No. Definitely not roasted chestnuts."

The earth trembled again and we scrambled to the treetops for a better view. My breathing hitched when I spotted a dozen demons marching toward the fae compound.

"Look at these guys," Liam said. "They didn't even bother to bring their A-game. I can kick Abaasy butts in my sleep." He blew a dismissive raspberry. "And check out those dingy swords and machetes. They look like someone snatched them from a museum. They're more like ornaments than weapons."

"This is it," I said. "This is the kick-off."

Saxon tensed. "Then we need to get to Belize. Now."

"We can't leave the fae to fight alone," I argued.

"They're not alone. Emil and Natasha are with them," Liam said.

"We're trying to convince them to join our coalition. I don't think they'll feel inclined if we abandon them in their hour of need," I pointed out.

"At least Evadne has weapons to spare," Liam said.

"What do these guys have in common?" I asked.

Liam's brow furrowed. "I don't think ugliness counts as weapon, unless you're talking about Martha Howard…"

"Liam, focus," Saxon barked.

The werevamp recovered his serious expression. "Sheesh. Relax, it's not like we're about to die." He paused to look down at the approaching demons. "Okay, I see your point."

"Iron," Evadne said. "The rest of you punks don't need to pay attention to that, but I do."

The fae had few weaknesses but iron was top of the list.

Saxon nodded gravely. "The Abaasy have iron teeth."

"And they have iron weapons," I said. "Trust me, those blades aren't new steel. That's why they look like artifacts."

"We need to make a move before they reach the compound," Purvis said.

Saxon spread his wings and vacated the branch and I followed suit. I landed in front of the first row of Abaasy. One of the demons swung his mace and I easily ducked out of the way.

"Use magic, Callie," Purvis called. "Why do you think we gave it to you?"

He was right. We had to hurry. The longer it took us to dispatch these demons, the more progress Varcin would make with his plan.

I'd developed a lot more skills since my first encounter with an Abaasy on the casino floor of Salt. In fact, that one Abaasy was the entire reason I was introduced to Pandora's Pride.

I considered using celestial fire to try to wipe them out in one blow, but the risk of causing a forest fire was too great. The fae wouldn't be too keen to help if I single-handedly destroyed their home.

Evadne fought beside me, alternating weapons. She seemed to be enjoying herself far more than she should. I may have been given the traits, but she was given the temperament.

I tapped into my fae powers and harnessed the light that filtered through the trees, using it to temporarily blind the demons in my path. They staggered around the forest, bumping into trees.

"Nice one," Evadne said.

My friends took advantage of the momentary blindness and managed to beat the demons into submission. I accessed my witch side and used magic to tie them together with vines and tree roots. The Abaasy struggled to free themselves, but they were no match for the mighty oak.

"Thank you. We'll take it from here," a regal voice said.

I turned and gasped. Rows of fae now stood outside the compound, along with their queen. Waves of red hair fell to her shoulders and she wore a suit of silver armor that coated her like liquid metal. The filtered sunlight cast a soft glow around her. I was so entranced that I almost didn't notice Emil and Natasha on either side of her.

"May I present Queen Mercy," Emil said.

We bowed our heads.

"It's an honor, Your Majesty," Purvis said.

"We are in your debt," the queen said. "Emil has informed us of an issue with some of our brethren. The Order of Beltane."

Evadne and I exchanged glances.

"You have my word that these warriors will no longer trouble you. I will make sure of it," the queen continued.

"Thank you, Your Majesty," Evadne said, lowering her head. "It's nice to know I'll no longer be hunted like an animal by my own kind."

I bit back a smile. Leave it to Evadne to look a gift horse in the mouth.

"I've also been informed of your need for our magic against a demon called Varcin," the queen said.

I raised my head to look at her. "Yes. Our plan involves stronger magic than we're capable of on our own. Without your help, it might not be possible."

The queen's gaze swept over the area. "And what if this Varcin sends more demons while I and my most powerful fae are aiding you? Who will defend our compound?"

Purvis stepped forward. "The alpha of the Midwest werewolf pack offers his assistance in your absence, Queen Mercy. The wolves will guard your territory like it's our own."

Queen Mercy balked. "How can I trust he will not attempt to acquire it for himself?"

Purvis held up his hand as though swearing an oath. "You have my word, Your Majesty. If the wolves act dishonorably, I'll deliver my own head on a spike."

The queen examined him for a long, agonizing moment and I worried that even the werewolf's offer wouldn't be enough to persuade her.

"Very well then," she finally said. "As the most powerful fae here, I offer you my services in defense of the realm."

I released the breath I'd been holding.

"When do you need me?" the queen asked. "I'll need time to prepare. It's been many years since I've left the compound."

It occurred to me that even though supernaturals had emerged from the shadows during the Plague, they'd still remained prisoners, too fearful of other supernaturals or losing power to travel and explore the rest of the world. Maybe that would change soon.

I hoped.

I glanced at the fallen Abaasy. "Unfortunately, I think time is a luxury we can no longer afford."

Emil bowed his head. "Callie's right, Your Majesty. As much as we'd like to give you time to prepare, that window has closed. We need you now."

CHAPTER SIXTEEN

"WHO DECIDED a jungle was the best place for an evil lair?" Liam grumbled as he pushed another hanging vine out of the way.

"It was good enough for the Mayans," Tate said with a shrug.

"I thought Varcin dehumidified this place," Evadne said. "My lungs suggest otherwise."

"I was already looking on the bright side that we ended up in the right place," Liam said. "You never know when Evadne's in charge of the portal."

"Keep it up and this can be a one-way trip," Evadne warned.

"I thought you're supposed to have better portal accuracy than Evadne," Liam said to me. "Why do we need to dodge lizards and the poop of howler monkeys?" He glanced up as though he was in imminent danger.

Natasha sliced through a vine with a machete. "Is this how Liam always acts in the field?"

"Pretty much," Tate said.

"In that case, I'm shocked he hasn't suffered an accidental death."

"This location was a deliberate choice," Purvis answered on my behalf. "You can't expect us to arrive right on the temple. We need the lay of the land first."

"And assess the number of demons we need to kill," Natasha added. She didn't look remotely unhappy about it.

"Remember to focus on the big picture," Saxon said, ignoring the gripes. He was back in leader mode. "We need Varcin. It doesn't matter how many lesser demons we slay, if we lose Varcin, we lose our shot at making this all go away."

Natasha halted, appearing to sense something. "Did anyone hear that?"

I paused to listen. I felt a presence in my mind but no actual voices. Telepathy was one of the traits I was reluctant to explore, mainly because I didn't want to know what others were thinking most of the time.

Evadne stopped walking and closed her eyes. "I hear voices in my head."

Liam snorted. "Why doesn't that surprise me?"

Evadne ignored him. "They're unintelligible, but we definitely have company."

Purvis inhaled deeply. "I smell cinnamon and nutmeg."

Liam chuckled. "Someone's hungry for pumpkin pie."

"I smell cloves," Evadne said.

"And ginger," I added.

Tate lit up. "It's allspice. There must be allspice trees up ahead."

Sure enough, we emerged from the oppressive jungle to an open area where a grove of trees was visible in the distance. The trees were tall and slender with whitish-grey trunks.

"I think we're almost there," I said.

Natasha's arm shot out to block me from progressing.

"We need recon before we go any further. It's too open out there. This place will be crawling with demons."

Purvis eyed Tate. "Are you ready with the invisibility spell?"

The witch nodded.

Natasha turned her sharp gaze to me. "Are the two fliers ready?"

Saxon's fingers brushed against mine. "Ready."

Tate focused on the two of us. Magic sparked in her palm as she prepared the spell.

"Remember, you'll be able to see each other but no one will be able to see you," Tate said.

"Your only job is to capture Varcin. Don't worry about any other demons you see," Natasha said. "I don't care how big and scary they are. Ignore them. If all goes according to plan, we'll eliminate them soon enough."

"We've got plenty of fighters waiting in the wings," Purvis said.

"And we're here for backup if anything goes wrong," Evadne added.

I knew it was killing the tri-brid that she wasn't the one being sent in to nab Varcin. Evadne wasn't one to enjoy the sidelines. Still, she seemed to take the decision in stride and was putting the needs of the team ahead of her own. Our little tri-brid was growing up.

"*Abscondo*," Tate said. Her open palm passed in front of us and I felt the precise moment that the spell washed over us. My whole body vibrated with magical energy.

"Good luck," Purvis said.

"We're all clear?" Saxon asked.

"All clear," Tate confirmed. "Can't see a single feather."

My eyes locked with Saxon and I tensed. We were about to enter the belly of the beast. Invisible or not, there was a chance we might not make it out alive. He must've been having the same thought because he hooked an arm around my waist and pulled me in for a kiss.

I tried not to think about the fact that this might be the last time we do this. The last time I smelled the salt on his skin or tasted the mint in his mouth. I had to think positive. I had to believe I'd made the right choices to get us here.

Reluctantly, I peeled myself off of him and took to the air before I could entertain any second thoughts. Saxon was beside me in an instant, a wing-length apart. El Castillo quickly came into view. The temple was about one hundred and thirty feet tall. More importantly, the structure was teeming with demons. Some were smaller and I suspected they were the minions that helped carry out the abduction plan at headquarters. They seemed to be occupied with another job at the moment that involved pulling ropes. As we flew closer, I realized they were using a pulley system to bring items to the top of the temple.

The temple itself was impressive. It was covered in carvings that would have been interesting to study if not for the mission. In the distance, I heard the call of howler monkeys. I wondered if they'd been disturbed by the influx of demons to their territory. Like many other areas, nature and its inhabitants had reclaimed parts of the world post-Plague.

Despite the number of demons populating the temple and its base, Varcin stood alone on the temple's apex. The demon seemed to be in the middle of a solitary ritual. He wore a purple cape affixed to a suit of black armor. He looked like a king preparing for battle. Appropriate and terrifying.

The moment we breached the ward, I felt the invisibility spell break. I hadn't expected a protective spell around the temple. Evadne and Tate would have to deal with that when they arrived at the base. It was a regrettable error. Varcin had proven to be a few steps ahead of us. We should've considered the possibility. If only we'd had more time...

Too late now.

As we landed behind him, he turned to look at us. His black eyes widened slightly at the sight of us.

"Sorry your plan didn't go according to…plan," Saxon said. He shot me a quick glance. "I'm glad Liam wasn't here to witness that."

Varcin gave us a nod of approval. "I'm impressed. It took us centuries to escape our prison, yet you managed it in a matter of days."

"You weren't as careful as you thought you were," Saxon said.

Varcin glowered. "Yes, I realize that. The fae was weak."

"Because she didn't want to help you. It was only to save her daughter."

"And is that why you're here now?" Varcin said simply. "To save her?"

I stiffened as the ugly reality settled in. The daughter was part of whatever ritual he was planning. I should've known.

"I need to appease the gods before I go in to battle, you see," Varcin explained. "And that requires a sacrifice."

"Newsflash, Varcin. The gods aren't listening," I said. "Even if they were, what makes you think they'd take your offering seriously? You're a demon they sealed away from this world. They're not going to support you taking over now."

"It's kill or be killed, isn't it?" Varcin said. "That's the state of the world you hold so dear. You've come to kill me before I can kill…" His mouth opened in what I assumed was an attempt at a smile. "Everyone else."

"That's where you're wrong, Varcin," Saxon said. "We haven't come to kill you. We've come to claim you."

The demon's black pools turned to slits. "I see you've brought friends."

From the top of the temple, I spotted werewolves running

toward the base of the temple. If the rest of our group was already in battle, I couldn't see them.

"We're stronger together," I said. "You should try it sometime."

Varcin laughed. "Maybe your little team is willing to band together, but the rest of the supernaturals only care for their own kind—and that will be their doom."

The demon struck the first blow, ramming his fist into Saxon's chest. The hybrid shot backward and nearly toppled over the edge of the temple, saved only by his wings.

Before Varcin could turn his attention to me, I responded in kind, landing a solid punch along his oddly-shaped jaw.

"That's pretty sexist of you, assuming he was the more powerful one," I said.

I didn't give the demon time to recover. I jumped onto his back and grabbed his arms to hold him in place. He surprised me by falling backward and smashing me against the stones.

I blinked rapidly to clear my blurry vision. Saxon was now preoccupied with several goblin-type demons—the same ones that had carried him off to the pocket realm.

Varcin sneered at me. "You are an insignificant creature. Do you really think you can take me down on your own?"

Part of me wanted to release celestial fire and end this now, but I knew I couldn't kill him. We had to keep him alive for the ritual—that was the only way we could truly end this. Otherwise, there would be another Varcin in a month or two, ready to kill scores of innocents and take over the world. Kill. Rinse. Repeat.

I leaped to my feet and accessed the potent magic that burned inside me. It only took nanoseconds here, thanks to the energy boost from the temple.

"*Impendiendum*," I shouted. I threw out my hands and white-hot light streaked from my fingertips. The force was so strong that it propelled me backward and I landed on my ass.

I watched as the white-hot light jolted Varcin and his body sparked. For a moment, I thought the spell didn't take. I had to give him credit; Varcin was tough. He was trying to fight the magic. He twitched and danced a few steps to the right. A few steps too far, in fact—

"Shit!" I spread my wings and launched into the air as Varcin veered over the side of the temple. I hooked my arm under his and heaved him back to the apex where he finally stopped moving.

Saxon kicked another goblin off the temple and regarded me. "Is the target secure?"

I motioned to a paralyzed Varcin. "What does it look like to you?"

At that moment, the rest of the team came barreling up the temple steps to reach us. Between the amount of blood and shredded clothing, they looked like they'd been through hell and back again. Liam held an unconscious young woman in his arms. She wore a white dress and a wreath of flowers circled her head.

"Looks like you found Courtney," I said.

"She was in a chamber below being prepped for sacrifice," Tate said.

"Good work," Purvis said, noticing Varcin on the floor.

I peeked over the side of the temple to see more demons congregating around us. "I wouldn't rest on any laurels yet."

Waves of new demons appeared at the base of the temple. The wolves were outnumbered.

"Ideas are welcome," Saxon said.

"That's supposed to be your job," Liam said. "You're the brains. I'm the muscle."

Tate groaned. "If that's the case, we're all in trouble."

"Callie, you'd better get started on that portal," Natasha

said. One of her arms was dislocated, a fang was broken, and her face was covered in bruises.

"On it." I kneeled on top of the temple and they formed a circle around me, facing outward.

"Tate, put a protective spell on her," Saxon ordered.

"Double up," Natasha said. "An inner one on her and an outer one for us. It might not hold, but it'll slow them down."

If worst came to worst, Saxon and I could fly away with Varcin, but we wouldn't be able to save everyone. Not the ideal solution.

"Hurry, Callie," Natasha snarled.

"They're coming," Tate said. Her voice trembled with fear.

"I'm working as fast as I can," I said. Portal creation took focus and added pressure only slowed me down.

Tate only managed to finish the spell around me when the nuisance demons launched their attack. I tried to stay focused on the portal and ignored the sounds of clashing metal and tearing flesh around me.

Out of the corner of my eye, Varcin began to stir. Terrific. I needed a longer timer on that spell. He was stronger than I realized.

"Secure Courtney and Varcin," Saxon yelled.

I centered myself and blocked out the noise. I needed to form the connection to the other side of the portal. Home would've been easy, but we weren't going home. Not yet.

I produced a pearl from my pocket that Abra had given to me to form the connection. She'd removed it from her favorite necklace and handed it to me in a tiny silk bag.

"How's that portal coming, Callie?" Natasha called.

I caught a glimpse of the vampire drenched in blood.

I turned back to the portal and poured my energy into the creation of the circle. The magic was there, but I was having trouble linking to the other side. I hoped there wasn't a problem on Abra's end. We couldn't afford any spanners in the works.

More demons crawled up the sides of the temple. They seemed adept at scaling without any need for steps.

"Buy me more time!" I started to panic. If I couldn't link us to the other axis mundi, we were going to die on this temple. The fate of the world depended on me right now. I may not like what the Pride had done to me, but the fact remained that, right here and now, I was the one equipped to handle this monumental task.

I would not—*could not*—fail.

"They're multiplying," I heard Tate say.

"Where are they coming from?" Liam asked. "They're coming straight out of the ground like some kind of mole demons."

Maybe they were. Varcin had managed to attract all types of demons to his hideout to carry out his plan. Unsurprising, given that he stood poised to take over the world.

Saxon moved into my line of vision and I gasped as a pink-skinned demon slashed one of the hybrid's wings with a rudimentary blade. Feathers flew in all directions and I winced at the sound of Saxon's agonizing moan.

My heart pounded as I reached again for the connection to Abra.

"Callie," Saxon yelled, his panic unmistakable.

A shadow passed overhead but I was too intent on the portal to look up.

"The angels," Liam said, sounding awestruck.

I glanced skyward to see a dozen angels in all their golden glory. Their white wings fanned out as they formed a protective circle above us.

"Doran came through," I murmured. And so would I. The thought spurred me on.

Celestial fire rained down one side of the temple and

demons fell to their deaths, screeching and wailing in protest. The angels wouldn't be able to set fire to the whole temple, not while we were on it. Still, their assistance was a huge help, alleviating the pressure and giving the team a chance to regroup.

I concentrated on the link as the circle glowed in front of me and felt the moment when it clicked into place.

"Yes," I shouted.

Saxon cast a glance at me over his shoulder. "Quick! Lower the shield," he ordered.

I heard the crackle of energy as the protective ward disintegrated. Liam arrived first, carrying Courtney. Purvis was close behind him with a semi-conscious Varcin.

"Go!" I herded each one through the portal.

The angels kept up the pressure from the air, but a demon managed to break through the celestial flames.

I didn't have a second to spare. Without a backward glance, I jumped headfirst through the portal.

CHAPTER SEVENTEEN

I ARRIVED on the other side of the portal, gasping for breath and my adrenaline pumping. The demon in hot pursuit of me landed beside me with a thud and a blade separated its body from its head before it had time to recover. I didn't stop to thank the supernatural with quick reflexes because I had to close the portal.

The moment I finished, an unseen hand helped me to my feet. I spun around to see Saxon grinning at me.

"You ready?" he asked.

"I assume that was your sword." I gestured to the demon head.

"Thought I'd wait by the portal and make sure nothing nasty got through. I tried to stop Evadne but…" He shrugged.

I smiled nervously. "Is everybody here?"

"Come and see."

I took a moment to get my bearings. Red rocks stretched as far as the eye could see. Sedona, Arizona. Another axis mundi. We did it. Well, most of it. Now we had to finish what we started.

Together we walked over the rise of the red hilltop and

there, intermingled with the members of Pandora's Pride, were well over one hundred fae and witches. The magical energy that vibrated from the group nearly knocked me off my feet.

I felt a soft hand on my shoulder. "It's really you." Marie appeared beside me in a sweeping dark blue cloak.

"You came." I could hardly contain my excitement.

"You were right, Callie. We have an obligation to others, even those outside the coven. We can't live in isolation forever."

I hugged her. "I'm so glad you're here. We need all the magic we can get."

Supernaturals parted so that I could reach the main event. On the apex of the hilltop was a dark pool of water. An enormous tree sprouted from its center with three huge branches. I noticed markings carved in the bark that reminded me of the carvings on the temple.

A tree with three branches, just like Marie's vision in the tea leaves, and in the heart of the tree shone the Sunstone. They must've used the stone to create the tree and the water and to forge the connection with the pocket realm. They'd been busy here, too.

It took me a moment to locate Varcin amidst the crowd. His slumped body was held upright by Emil and Evadne at the edge of the pool. As though sensing my presence, his head lifted and he looked me directly in the eye.

"What is this?" the demon asked. His gaze swept the crowd. "All of you are here for me?" His laugh was raspy and mocking. "You left many demons behind. Do you plan to bring each one of us here and drown us?" He eyed the witches. "I would think you of all supernaturals would object to that."

Abra ignored his remark. "As you can see, on the trunk of this tree we've carved runes that symbolize each species."

"We've also carved the fate of you and your friends on the branches," Emil added, "which will solidify your destiny."

Varcin spat in the pool and the water steamed where his saliva landed.

I thought of Esther's final words to me. *Sometimes you need to destroy in order to create.* We were about to destroy the Plague demons and start the world anew again.

Abra instructed everyone to join hands. Supernaturals gathered closer, forming a complete circle around the pool of water.

The witches began to chant first and everyone else joined in once they understood the words.

Magic hummed around me. It seemed to be everywhere all at once. Within me. Around me. From the sky all the way to the underworld, I felt its effects. It was glorious.

"*Reposco*," Abra said, loud enough for all to hear.

"*Reposco*," we all repeated.

The water rippled. Emil and Evadne pushed Varcin forward and the demon plunged into the water, disappearing in its depths.

Abra looked at Saxon. "Make the call."

He already held a phone in his hand and tapped the screen.

"Who are you calling?" I whispered.

"Nita has eyes on several Plague demons. We want her to confirm they're gone." He paused. "Anything?"

I could hardly stand the anticipation.

Saxon frowned. "Thanks, I'll let them know." He tucked away the phone. "Still there."

A collective groan followed his announcement.

"But we made the sacrifice," Liam said. "That's supposed to seal the deal."

I stared at the tree, remembering the story of Odin.

"No," I said. "We didn't. Varcin wasn't the sacrifice. He

was the physical link between realms. This spell requires *our* sacrifice. Odin had to give his own eye, not someone else's. Only then was he was permitted to drink from the Well of Urd and gain the knowledge he wanted."

Tate stared into the depths of the murky water. "Then Varcin isn't our offering."

A weight settled in the pit of my stomach as the realization swept over me. One last hurdle.

"Why do I get the feeling we need to offer more than an eye?" Liam said, edging away from the water.

"Calandra is correct," Abra said. "I was hoping it might not be necessary given all the magic at our disposal, but I can see that, without it, the spell will fail."

I gritted my teeth to keep from screaming. Abra knew this whole time that a sacrifice would likely be required. Why didn't it surprise me that she kept the news to herself?

"You knew and you didn't tell us?" Evadne asked, exasperated.

"As I said, I was hoping it wouldn't be necessary," the witch said. "I chose to err on the side of caution."

Evadne waved a hand. "So now what? We fail because we haven't prepared a sacrifice?"

"We don't need to prepare it," Abra said. "We only need to give it now to complete the spell. As long as the tree and water are still here, we have time."

"What if we're wrong?" Tate asked, her eyes shining. "What if we go through all this—the Sunstone, a sacrifice— and it doesn't work?"

"Then it will have been for the worthiest of causes," Abra said.

I stepped forward, my heart thundering in my chest. "It's me," I said. "I never should've existed in the first place. It makes sense that I should be the sacrifice."

"No!" Saxon grabbed my arm with such force, he nearly

pulled it from its socket. Fear and panic radiated from him in a way I'd never seen in battle.

I tried to keep my composure. "Think about it, Saxon. I should've died as a baby. I wouldn't have survived if the Pride hadn't found me. These years were all a bonus."

"But they did find you," he said. "And they saved you." He loosened his grip on me.

"And then you went on to save countless others," Tate added.

I gazed at the water below. "And now I can save millions more with one simple act."

"It's far from simple," Saxon said.

"Who else do you suggest?" I asked.

"Me," he said. "I'll do it."

Evadne elbowed her way forward. "Everybody's a hero today. Screw that, if anyone dies for glory, it's going to be me. I would've died, too, if it weren't for the Pride."

We were all so busy arguing that we failed to see the older witch take her place at the rim on the opposite side of the pool, too far for anyone to reach her in time.

"My time has come," Abra said, so softly that the words took a moment to register. "I have achieved everything I set out to do, thanks to all of you. It is time for me to take my leave."

"No," Tate said. "Absolutely not."

Abra's cloak swirled around her ankles as a gentle breeze blew through. "Tate, my dear. I'll always be with you."

Before the older witch could move, I retracted my wings and jumped.

I plunged feet first into the cold water. For a moment, it seemed that space and time ceased to exist. That *I* ceased to exist. Then the darkness receded and I was met with a bright light that lessened until I could see a silhouette hovering beside me. The shadowy figure took on a more solid form—a form I knew well.

Dad?

Lark.

I advanced toward him, my movements heavy and inelegant. It was as though the air itself resisted me.

He looked younger somehow, with the shaggy haircut I remembered from my adolescence.

Dad, is it really you?

You don't belong here, Lark. You must go back.

It's a sacrifice, Dad. Now I can be with you.

The shake of his head seemed to happen in slow motion. *Today isn't that day.*

But this is how I save the world. I chose the right paths and now my job is done.

Your job may be done, Lark, but your life is far from over.

He wrapped his arms around me and I relished the moment. He kissed my cheek with a tenderness he'd never offered in his lifetime, always too busy with teachable moments. Before I could react, I felt his arms propel me upward.

No!

His image below me faded, blending with the inky water. Strong fingers curled around my wrist and pulled. I broke through the surface of the water and coughed.

"No," I sputtered.

Saxon hovered in the air above the water, his huge wings casting shadows around me. He held my arm with a firm grip and flew to the safety at the side of the water.

"I don't understand. Why didn't I sink?"

"Abra stopped you," Saxon said. "She managed to cast a spell on you before you even hit the water."

"I'm old, but I'm far from slow," the witch said.

I glared at her. "Why would you do that?"

Abra looked at me with affection. "Because you've sacrificed enough for the greater good, Calandra Wendell. And now it's my turn."

Abra was mentally prepared for this moment. She must've decided she would be the one to go back when she realized a sacrifice might be necessary. She cast an immobilization spell so quickly that no one had time to protect themselves.

The witch didn't jump. She simply took a step forward and stepped into the water with the same elegance and grace she exhibited when conjuring a spell or advising the team of a mission.

No one made a move to stop her—because we couldn't. Her magic wasn't strong enough at this point to hold us for very long—she'd used too much of it for the main event—but she only needed a moment. By the time the spell weakened to sufficiently break through it, she was gone.

Tate dropped to her knees at the edge of the pool and made a choking sound. I seemed stuck in place, still dripping wet and staring at the spot where her head had fully submerged.

"Good-bye, old friend," Natasha said. I'd never seen the vampire close to tears before. Somehow that realization saddened me even more.

The water began to bubble and we backed away. Tate rose to her feet and watched in awe as the tree shook. I pulled her by the shoulder, away from the edge. Whatever was about to happen, I didn't want to lose her, too.

"It's working," Doran said.

"I hope so, or all this was for nothing." Evadne crossed her arms, almost daring the spell to fail.

The tree started to glow from within and each branch vibrated with magical energy. Everyone clasped hands again as the tree sank into the water. I watched with tears streaming down my cheeks as the last branch was swallowed by the liquid blackness. Once the tree was gone, the water seeped into the red earth and dissipated, leaving us around a shallow crater.

Saxon called Nita again. This time, whatever she said prompted a broad smile from the hybrid.

"It's done," he yelled. "They're gone."

The witches and fae cheered and hugged each other. I spotted Queen Mercy hugging Lloyd. I marveled at the number of fae and witches in the same space. At the vampires who came to our aid. The werewolves and angels who came all the way to Belize to help us. No arguing. No avoidance. They'd worked together—with us—and ended the Plague.

The Pride thought they needed to find a way to create super soldiers, to unite all the powers into one being, but they were wrong. They only needed to find a way to unite all the beings.

A burst of steam emanated from the crater before blowing away with the wind.

"That's it," Tate said in disbelief. "No more Plague demons."

"No more pocket realm either," Liam added.

"We destroyed a realm," Evadne said, smirking. "That's badass."

I stared at the crater, wishing Abra everlasting peace and love. "It seems we're the gods now."

CHAPTER EIGHTEEN

I SLIPPED OUT of my room at Salt early the next morning and walked across the boardwalk to the beach. There was no one as far as the eye could see, not even a seagull.

There was no one.

My biological parents were long gone. My father was gone. Even the mighty Abra was no longer with us. But we'd saved *millions* of lives and we'd altered the world order—again. Humans still had supernaturals to contend with, of course, but hopefully the absence of Plague demons would give everyone a fresh start.

I stood on the beach with my toes buried in the sand and let the new reality sink in. The waves rolled an inch from my feet before being summoned back to the ocean. The sun inched its way to the horizon and I gazed at the ribbons of golden light streaming from its blurred edges.

I sensed a presence behind me and waited.

"Poker chip for your thoughts."

I glanced down and saw a red and white chip resting in Saxon's open palm.

"Is that worth more or less than a penny?" I asked, smiling. I took the chip and slipped it into my pocket.

"Depends on whether you're feeling lucky." He stepped in line with me, his boots covered in wet sand.

"I couldn't sleep. Figured I might as well enjoy a beautiful sunrise," I said.

"It's a privilege, isn't it? To live to see another one."

I knew he was thinking of everyone we'd lost. So was I.

"I can't stop wondering how the world will change in another thirty years," I said. "Will humans migrate back to places they'd abandoned? Will we get to experience a taste of the pre-Plague life that we were denied?"

"That's the exciting part of uncertainty, I guess," he said. "We'll have to wait and see."

I thought of all the stories my father had shared with me about life before the Plague. The world hadn't been perfect, of course, but it hadn't been filled with the same level of fear and discord that Plague demons had brought with them.

"Where do you think you'll go next?" he asked.

"Funny you should ask. That's what I've been trying to decide."

He clasped my hand and gave it a gentle squeeze. "You're not alone, Callie. Not if you don't want to be."

"What about you?" I asked, almost afraid to hear the answer.

"I don't know. I was hoping whatever it is, we'd be doing it together."

I could've melted into the ocean. I moved into his arms and we shared a long, lingering kiss that left me in no doubt as to his feelings for me.

"Are you sure about this?" he asked. "About me? If you want to take your time, maybe get out there in the world first, I'd understand."

I slapped my palms flat against his chest. "If there's one thing I've learned, it's that life is precious and fleeting and you should spend it with the ones who matter most." I stood on the tips of my toes kissed him again. "You, Saxon Hanley, matter most."

Tate appeared beside us wrapped warmly in a fur-lined hoodie. Her hands were stuffed deep inside the pockets. "I guess I wasn't the only one who couldn't sleep."

"How are you?" I asked. It couldn't have been easy for her, watching her grandmother submit to death.

The young witch shrugged. "It'll take time."

"I hope it doesn't take too long because there's a roulette wheel with my name on it inside one of these casinos." Liam wandered across the beach clad in pajama bottoms and a grey Salt sweatshirt.

"Gambling?" I queried. "That's how you intend to spend your first day of freedom?"

"I figured I'd ease into normalcy. Besides, I'm feeling lucky after everything we've been through. Aren't you?"

He wasn't wrong. I felt extremely lucky.

"You must be feeling lucky if you're wearing a Salt sweatshirt in close proximity to Sweetie's," Tate said, angling her head toward the boardwalk.

"Haven't you heard? The feud's over," Saxon said. "They've decided to work together and unite the territories."

Tate's eyes rounded. "Wow. I think that might actually be the most miraculous thing that's happened this week."

"Not so fast."

I turned to see Evadne trotting toward us. "I think the five of us standing here in one piece qualifies as the most miraculous thing that's happened this week." She joined us at the water's edge.

"What will you do now?" Tate asked the tri-brid.

Evadne kicked a shell into the oncoming wave. "Haven't decided. I haven't had the luxury of choices before."

"Me neither," Tate said. "I'm considering law enforcement for an international agency."

"Basically, you want to keep doing the same job for a different boss?" Evadne blew a raspberry. "No thanks."

Tate bristled. "It wouldn't be the same. There won't be Plague demons, but there will always be supernatural crime to squelch."

"Squelch." Liam chuckled. "You make it sound so dainty."

"What about you, werevamp?" Evadne asked. "Think you'll stay local?"

Liam cast a glance over his shoulder at the row of beckoning buildings. "I don't know. I think I'll travel for a bit and then decide. Honestly, if you guys aren't here, I don't know that I'd call this home anymore."

"Aw, that's both pathetic and sweet," Evadne chided him.

"Is this the part where you two announce you'll be getting married at the nearest chapel and raising your freaky brood of kids in suburbia?" Liam asked.

I laughed. "What makes you think we'd choose suburbia? Our freaky kids would be more at home in the mountains."

Liam's jaw dropped. "I was joking. You're not seriously getting married, are you?"

Saxon smirked. "Callie knows I'm a patient guy."

"Will you stay here?" Evadne asked. "I'd like to know where to find you in case I get myself into a jam I can't get out of."

Saxon snaked his arm along my waist. "We're taking a trip to the Rockies. Callie wants to show me where she grew up."

I swiveled toward him. "I do?"

He grinned. "You do."

Liam shivered. "No thanks. Too cold and full of altitude."

"It's one of the most beautiful places on earth," I said. "You're missing out."

Liam raised a hand. "Seeing as you two have wings, I call dibs on the van."

Tate moaned. "You're welcome to it."

"Seriously," Evadne said. "I wouldn't be caught dead in that thing."

"It feels like we've been awake for hours," Tate said. "Should we go to a diner? I think that one on New York Avenue is open early."

"No need. I brought supplies," Evadne said.

I turned to look, half expecting to see a cache of weapons. I smiled when I saw her produce a bottle of champagne from the deep recess of her hoodie pocket.

"Breakfast of champions," she added.

"If I drink this on an empty stomach, you'll all regret it," I warned.

Liam reached into his pocket and produced a handful of chestnuts. "I was saving these for an emergency. I guess this qualifies."

I took a few chestnuts as Evadne raised the bottle toward the sun. "To a new day. May we survive many more." She pulled out the cork with her fang and everyone scattered as the bubbly spilled out of the top.

Liam swiped the bottle and took a swig. "To good friends. There's no one else I'd rather have by my side in a fight to the death." He passed the bottle to Tate.

"To those we lost," the witch said. She drank and handed the bottle to Saxon.

"And to those we love," the hybrid said, his mismatched eyes pinned on me. He swallowed a few gulps and passed the bottle to me.

"To family," I said. "Those by blood, those by choice, and those by magic."

"Cheers," they said in unison.

I tipped back the bottle, enjoying the tickle of the bubbles as they passed down my throat, and drank to the dawn of a new era.

ALSO BY ANNABEL CHASE

A Magic Bullet series
Burned
Death Match
Demon Hunt
Soulfire

Spellslingers Academy of Magic
Outcast, Warden of the West, Book 1
Outclassed, Warden of the West, Book 2
Outlast, Warden of the West, Book 3

Outlier, Sentry of the South, Book 1
Outfox, Sentry of the South, Book 2
Outbreak, Sentry of the South, Book 3

Outwit, Enforcer of the East, Book 1
Outlaw, Enforcer of the East, Book 2

Outrun, Keeper of the North, Book 1
Outgrow, Keeper of the North, Book 2